INCARNATION

I0653863

# INCARNATION
## A Kid Sensation Novel


By


Kevin Hardman

# INCARNATION

Cover Design by Isikol

Edited by Faith Williams, The Atwater Group

This book is published by I&H Recherche Publishing.

ISBN: 978-1-937666-46-0

Printed in the U.S.A.

# INCARNATION

Mariner chuckled. "There's an old saying among our kind: Incarnates don't have enemies."

I frowned. "What's that supposed to mean?"

"Enemy implies an adversary," Endow explained. "Someone or something capable of competing with you or doing you harm. Gamma was an Incarnate."

"And because almost nothing can harm an Incarnate, you don't have enemies," I concluded. "There's a fallacy in that logic, but we'll come back to that. For now, though, I'll phrase the question a little differently: who didn't like her?"

"She wielded almost limitless power for eons," said an odd, almost robotic voice. "There would be many who did not like her."

I looked around in bewilderment. I hadn't seen anyone speak. In addition, the voice had seemed to come from all around us.

I reached out to Rune telepathically. <What the hell was that?>

<Reverb,> he responded. <He speaks by taking ambient sound – the rustle of cloth, the squeak of a chair, even breath sounds – and playing around with things like modulation and tonality until he obtains a reverberation approximating the word he wants.>

<Seems like a lot of work,> I surmised. <Why doesn't he just speak?>

<Because the sound of his voice would kill you.>

# INCARNATION

# INCARNATION

## ACKNOWLEDGMENTS

I would like to thank the following for their help with this book: as always, GOD first, since He's the architect behind any success I experience; my loving family, who have always supported me; and my readers, who continue to encourage me with their generous praise.

# INCARNATION

Thank you for purchasing this book! If, after reading, you find that you enjoyed it, please feel free to leave a review on the site from which it was purchased.

Also, if you would like to be notified when I release new books, please subscribe to my mailing list via the following link: http://eepurl.com/C5a45

Finally, for those who may be interested in following me, I have included my website and social media account info:

Website: http://www.kevinhardmanauthor.com/

BookBub: https://www.bookbub.com/authors/kevin-hardman

Amazon: https://amazon.com/author/kevinhardman

Facebook: www.facebook.com/kevin.hardman.967

Twitter: @kevindhardman

# Chapter 1

We popped up in a field — a wide swath of acreage filled with what looked like stalks of grain. If grain were blue, that is, and produced soft musical tones when the wind blew. It was an immediate indication that we weren't anywhere close to a place I'd call "home."

"Where are we?" I asked, already knowing that we were no longer on Earth.

"That's a little tricky to answer," said my companion, Rune. "It's not really a spot you can plot on a map — or pin down temporally."

I frowned. "I take it this is one of those places beyond the conventional bounds of the universe — outside of space and time."

"Something like that," Rune replied. As he spoke, a bevy of unusual symbols and designs — the source of his moniker — moved eerily across the surface of his skin. It was an effect that most people found creepy.

I let out a slight groan of exasperation.

"What?" Rune said in mock surprise. "Did I fail to mention that we'd be going off-site?"

"Off-*site*?" I repeated skeptically. "This isn't off-site. This isn't even off-*planet*. There's no word for what this is."

Rune seemed to ruminate on this for a second, then grinned. "How about 'off-cosmos'?"

"Feels like an understatement," I replied, noting that I was being subjected to my companion's sense of humor. "When you asked for my help, you didn't say anything about dragging me off to this literal Limbo."

Rune laughed. "Well, would it have made a difference if I had?"

I shrugged, then grudgingly admitted, "Probably not."

"That's what I thought," Rune stated with a nod. "Besides, it's not like you haven't experienced this before."

I didn't say anything as I reflected on Rune's comment. He was referring to the fact that he and I had had a previous misadventure wherein we found ourselves in a similar realm outside of space and time. It was then that I'd become aware of Rune's true nature.

As far as most people knew, Rune was a member of the Alpha League (Earth's greatest superhero team) and was generally considered something along the lines of a sorcerer or magician. On his part, Rune never disabused anyone of the notion and even went along with it, such as dressing the part by occasionally wearing a wizard's robe (as he was now) and carrying a magician's staff. In truth, however, Rune was far more than that. He was an Incarnate — the physical embodiment of certain potent forces and powers.

As evidence of this, there was the fact that Rune had brought us from my bedroom to our current location with a mere snap of his fingers. Now that I thought about it, I realized that it had been around midnight when we left, but it now seemed to be daylight. I glanced up, expecting to see something like two suns, an array of planetary bodies, or something along those lines.

Initially, I saw nothing out of the ordinary — fluffy white clouds floating against a backdrop of expansive blue sky. Without warning, however, the scene changed. It was as if I was looking at a reversible figure — one of those optical illusions whereby the same image can appear to be

# INCARNATION

two different things (such as when the same drawing can look like an old woman when viewed from one angle, and like a young woman when observed from another). In this instance, I'd originally been looking up at the wild blue yonder when it seemingly morphed into one of the most stunning spectacles I'd ever laid eyes on.

Above us, staring down, was a crowd of giants.

No, not giants — titans.

No, even that was an incredibly flawed and deficient description.

Frankly speaking, there was no word I could think of — colossus, Goliath, Polypheme, what have you — that could adequately describe the stature, the sheer magnitude, of the beings around us.

They looked like people — albeit people who had grown to a height that could only be measured in miles. Their heads weren't in the clouds; they were literally above them. Well above them. Their bodies were equally massive, each easily as wide as a metropolis.

They were so gargantuan that I instinctively realized in the back of my mind that there was no way they were standing on solid ground — there wouldn't have been room for them. Instead, their towering forms extended down toward terra firma but seemed to visually dissolve around the horizon. All in all, it was as if the realm or dimension Rune had brought us to were a snow globe, with a bunch of people standing around watching it. (In truth, it felt like any one of them could simply reach out and palm us like a basketball if they so desired.) However, they didn't move — didn't even appear to breathe. From all appearances, they were statues.

Somewhat in shock, I took a step back, essentially mesmerized by the scale of what I was looking at.

"Wh-what…?" I mumbled, spinning slowly in a circle and noting that the immense beings were all around us. "How…?"

I felt more than saw Rune staring at me intently, although with my peripheral vision I observed him following my gaze.

"Wait," he muttered, sounding a little surprised. "You can see that?"

Not quite able to find my tongue, I simply nodded emphatically.

Out of the corner of my eye, I saw Rune make a vague gesture. Instantly, the images vanished, replaced by what could be described as normal sky.

The visual change seemed to bring me back to myself. I inhaled deeply, suddenly realizing that I had been holding my breath.

Rune gave me a once-over. "You good?"

"Yeah," I replied with a nod. "Just caught a little off guard. What were those things?"

"Incarnates," Rune answered.

I stared at him in surprise. "What — all of them?"

"Yeah — including the good-looking dude with the impeccable taste in clothes," Rune said with a smile.

"Huh?" I muttered with a frown.

Rune traced an imaginary square in the air with his forefinger. Unexpectedly, something like a window appeared, and within it I saw the giants again. Like a camera, my companion's window zoomed in on one of the behemoths. Much to my surprise (and ignoring its size), I noted that it did indeed appear to be Rune, and was even dressed as he was. Apparently I had been so startled by the titans that I hadn't even noticed that he was among them, so to speak.

# INCARNATION

I turned to my companion, confusion evident on my face. "Why is there a colossal statue of you looming over this place?"

"It's not a statue," Rune declared flatly.

Bewildered, I looked back at the window and was surprised to see the image of Rune wink at me. A moment later, while I was still trying to process what I'd just observed, the window vanished. Brow creased, I simply stared at Rune, a million questions bubbling in my brain, with each jockeying for position in order to be the first out of my mouth.

"It all ties into why I brought you here," he said, before I could ask anything. "Why I need your help."

"Which is what?" I asked.

"We have a mystery on our hands that, truthfully, is unprecedented."

"What type of mystery?"

"The impossible has happened," Rune answered in a no-nonsense tone. "An Incarnate has been murdered."

## Chapter 2

"What do you mean, 'murdered'?" I asked after getting over my surprise. "I thought Incarnates were all-powerful."

"We're not *all*-powerful, but we come pretty close," Rune stated. "That said, being powerful doesn't necessarily equate to being immortal, although you're not that far off-base. As I mentioned, this has never happened before. Up until now, I don't think any of us felt it *could* happen."

"What — one of you getting killed?"

Rune nodded. "Yes, although, all things considered, we should have been aware of the possibility — especially in *this* place."

"This place?" I repeated.

Rune spread his arms wide, making an all-encompassing gesture. "This realm is known as Permovren. Incarnates are required to come here occasionally, although doing so makes us vulnerable."

I frowned. "You're going to have to explain that."

Rune appeared pensive for a moment, then said, "When we Incarnates come here, it is not with the incorporation of our full slate of powers. The effigies you saw…" He trailed off and pointed up toward the sky.

"You mean the titans?" I interjected.

"Yeah," he acknowledged. "They're a physical manifestation of the bulk of our powers. Their magnitude, as opposed to our apparent size when in Permovren, is a reflection of the potency we leave vested in them versus what we bring into this dimension with us."

My brow furrowed as Rune's words rolled around in my head. "So you're saying this place has something akin to a mystical or metaphysical metal detector, with the end result being that you have to check your powers at the door."

"Pretty much," Rune said. "And pick them up on the way out."

I spent a moment thinking about the sheer size of the "effigies," as Rune referred to them, and juxtaposed that to his current appearance. "So does that mean you don't have any of your powers here?"

Rune laughed and then clapped his hands together once. Instantly and simultaneously, a dozen bolts of lightning — accompanied by the earsplitting sound of thunder — struck the ground in a circle around us. I managed to avoid starting as the lightning flashed, but the proximity of the thunder made me wince. The entire episode was a testament to the fact that, even if the vast majority of his powers were inaccessible, my companion was still not someone to be trifled with.

"Any more questions?" Rune asked with a grin.

# INCARNATION

## Chapter 3

I actually did have more questions — first and foremost among them being whether the Incarnates' mystical metal detector had stripped me of any of *my* powers. I decided to do a quick sound check by dashing around the grain field at super speed, teleporting around it, and then flying into the air above it. Finding that those three abilities were still functioning (along with Rune's solemn promise that the "metal detector" was only for Incarnates), I eschewed testing *all* of my powers and went on the assumption that everything was in working order.

That said, there were still a ton of things I needed to quiz Rune about. However, he asked that I hold off on any more questions for the nonce.

"Wait until we get inside and get settled," he said.

Befuddled, I glanced around, still seeing nothing but stalks of blue grain.

"Inside where?" I finally asked.

Smiling, Rune pointed with his chin to a point over my shoulder. Turning around, I unexpectedly found myself at the bottom of a lengthy set of steps leading up to the double doors of a huge castle.

\*\*\*\*\*\*\*\*\*\*\*\*\*\*\*\*\*\*\*\*\*\*\*\*\*\*\*\*\*\*\*\*\*\*\*\*\*\*\*

"What is this place?" I asked as Rune and I went up the stairs.

"Castle Permovren," Rune replied, as if it were obvious.

"I mean, where did it come from?"

"Honestly, it was always there," he said. "It just didn't materialize until we were ready to go in."

# INCARNATION

"I would have liked to have been inside when the lightning struck," I declared.

Rune chuckled. "Those thunderbolts were purely for effect, with no ability to do actual harm — except maybe to eardrums."

I was about to comment, but at that moment we reached the top of the steps and the double doors opened. Standing there, dressed in blue-and-gray livery like some kind of majordomo, was a tall fellow with a thick black beard and long braided hair.

"Welcome back, *Chomarsus*," the apparent majordomo said to Rune. "It has been too long since you graced us with your presence."

"Too true, Dalmion," Rune replied as we stepped inside. "Too true."

Looking around, I saw that we were in a large foyer, with hallways and corridors branching off in numerous directions. Although the castle was obviously sizable — something I'd been able to discern while we were outside — the interior was very different than what I anticipated in terms of decorations. In essence, I had been expecting lavish furnishings, expensive artwork, marble columns, and more. Instead, the interior was essentially drab and unadorned, with everything I saw reflecting rather simple tastes.

"Ah," Dalmion muttered, looking at me as he closed the doors. "I see you have finally acquired a *laamuffal*."

"Uh…" Rune droned, glancing at me. "Something like that."

"Excellent," the majordomo said with a smile. "It's well past time."

I frowned. "What's a llama-ful?"

"You don't know?" Dalmion asked, looking surprised. "Well, it's—"

"We'll be heading to my suite now," Rune cut in. "Thank you, Dalmion."

"Of course, *Chomarsus*," Dalmion said, inclining his head slightly. "Please call on me if I can be of service."

With that, Dalmion left us.

"Come on," Rune said, and began walking down one of the hallways.

Falling into step beside him, I asked, "So, what was that word that guy — Dalmion — used back there?"

"*Chomarsus*?" Rune intoned. "It's just a colloquial term for an Incarnate."

I shook my head. "No, not that. The other word — llama-ful."

"*Laamuffal*," Rune corrected, putting the accent on the middle syllable. "It, uh, it just means that you're here with me."

"You mean like your guest?"

"Sure, yeah. Like that."

I didn't say anything, but had my empathic senses turned up to the max. As was often the case with Rune, I didn't really detect anything, but my gut was telling me there was more to the story.

"And here we are," Rune announced, interrupting my thoughts.

I looked up, and then turned to my companion, baffled. We had stopped in front of a bare wall, about ten feet in height and stretching about fifteen feet to either side of us.

Ignoring my befuddlement, Rune tapped the middle of the wall with the end of his staff. At the place where his staff made contact, a bright amber-colored dot appeared. Almost immediately, the dot began extending itself in a vertical line, simultaneously heading for the floor and the ceiling. When it reached those two junctures, the line split and began running horizontal — to the right and left — at both ends.

By this time, I had an inkling of what was happening, and my suspicions were proven correct a moment later when the line's split ends all began running vertical again, with the two at the ceiling heading down and the two at the floor cruising up. Seconds later, the ends of the line all joined, framing the contours of two conjoined rectangles before flashing brightly and disappearing.

Rune put out a hand and pushed on the center line between the two rectangles, which I now recognized as doors. They swung inward easily, revealing a large, lavish apartment that was easily on par with the penthouse or presidential suite of any luxury hotel. Stepping in, we found ourselves surrounded by opulence on all sides, from vaulted ceilings to posh furnishings to marble floors to a baby grand piano. It was in stark contrast to what I had observed during our jaunt through the castle, and I said as much to Rune as the doors closed behind us.

"If you wield enough power," he stated in response, "for a long enough time, you'll quickly realize that appearances are quite often immaterial — especially in terms of possessions. What really matters is comfort and utility. A solid gold chair might look good and seem impressive, but sitting it in all day would be dolorous. A good old recliner would be much more relaxing."

I thought about this for a moment. "So you're saying that Incarnates have evolved beyond being impressed by gaudy displays of wealth and power."

"What I'm saying is that it's hard to be impressed when almost nothing is beyond your reach," Rune explained. "If you're a billionaire, you aren't wowed if one of your peers buys a ten-year-old station wagon. You can just go buy one of your own — or a thousand, if you're really into that kind of thing."

"And to you guys, *everything's* a ten-year-old station wagon," I surmised.

"Not everything, but…" He trailed off, shrugging.

"So why all this?" I asked, gesturing toward our opulent surroundings. "Why outfit this place as the lap of luxury if you don't care about appearances?"

Rune's eyebrows went up in surprise. "You don't like it?"

"I think it's great," I replied. "It's actually…"

My words came to a halt and I frowned as a new thought occurred to me, based on the discussion we'd just had.

"Wait a minute," I muttered, glancing around at our lavish accommodations. "Is all of this for *my* benefit?"

Rune gave a somewhat hesitant nod. "Since I asked for your help, I thought it only fitting that I put you up in style."

"I appreciate it, but it wasn't necessary."

"Consider it a small token of my esteem," Rune said. "Anyway, moving on to more important issues." He pointed toward a wooden door set in a wall on one side of the room and declared, "My quarters." He pointed to the opposite wall that was home to a similar door. "Your quarters. Everything else can be considered a common area."

"Works for me," I said, flopping down onto a plush couch. "Now, can you give me a little more detail about what's going on here?"

Rune took a seat in an easy chair across from me. "It's just as I said. An Incarnate was murdered."

"How did it happen?" I asked.

A look of concern settled on my companion's face. "We're not sure."

I blinked in surprise. "What do you mean you're not sure?"

"Exactly what I said. We're not sure what happened to her."

"Meaning you're not sure how she died."

"Correct."

"Well, what kind of condition was the body in?"

Rune pursed his lips, seeming to concentrate for a moment before responding. "There's no real way to answer that."

"Sure there is," I insisted. "If a body was shot, it has bullet holes. If it was stabbed, it has knife wounds. Basically, the condition of the body can tell you what happened to it. You can pick that up from any detective show."

"Agreed," Rune murmured. "The problem is, there wasn't a body."

I frowned. "No body?"

"Nope," Rune said.

"So how do you know she's dead?" I asked.

"Well, aside from being Incarnates and having the ability to innately sense it, there's also the fact that her effigy crumbled."

"Her effigy?" I repeated with a frown — and then remembered. "Oh — the giant statues."

"Yeah," Rune said. "It basically disintegrated."

"So you're connected," I concluded. "You and your effigy."

Rune nodded. "As I mentioned before, it's a manifestation of the bulk of my power. The part of me that you're seeing right now represents my core — the essence of my being."

"So this part of you that I'm talking to is like the life spark of Rune the Incarnate."

He laughed. "Something like that, although it's probably easier to think of the 'me' in here as the brain and the effigy as the body."

"But while you're in here, you're vulnerable," I noted, remembering what Rune had said earlier. "And if you kill the brain…"

I didn't finish, but Rune, sobering instantly, knew exactly where my thoughts had been headed.

"If you kill the brain," he echoed, "the body will die."

"Okay, so what's my role in all this?"

"Isn't it obvious?" Rune asked in surprise. "You're here to find the murderer."

# INCARNATION

## Chapter 4

"Hold on," I almost shouted, sitting up. "I'm not a detective. Solving murders isn't what I do."

"Sure it is," Rune countered. "How many times have you had to figure out what villain was killing people and find a way to stop him?"

I frowned. "That's not quite the same thing."

"I don't see a distinction. Murder is murder, whether it's done by a normal person, a supervillain, or an Incarnate."

"Well, that sort of begs the question: how do you kill one of you guys?"

"Not easily, that's for sure," Rune stated, clearly concentrating on the question. "Even with*out* most of our *sivrrut*."

"*Sivrrut?*" I repeated, unsure what he was talking about.

"It's a term used to describe the power of an Incarnate," he explained. "Now, with respect to how we can be killed, the only thing absolutely certain is that only another Incarnate could do it."

"So one of you is a killer."

"So it would seem."

"I guess now's a time to ask a question I hadn't focused on before," I said. "Exactly how many of you guys are there?"

Rune appeared to reflect for a moment. "I'm not sure how to answer that."

I gave him a skeptical look. "Is there something tricky about the question?"

# INCARNATION

"Our numbers aren't set. That said, there's never more than a score of us, and at the moment we number about a dozen. But a new Incarnate can arise at any time."

"Well, how does someone become an Incarnate?"

"I can't tell you that," Rune declared, almost apologetically.

"Oh, come on," I moaned in exasperation. "You've got to know the answer to that one. You're an Incarnate yourself."

"It's not that I don't know," Rune explained. "It's that I'm forbidden to tell you."

I gave him a look of incomprehension, which led him to expound.

"It's a bit like the California gold rush," he said, "when people went completely bananas trying to strike it rich. Likewise, if you show them the path to almost limitless power, they'll do unthinkable things and take insane risks to obtain it."

I nodded in understanding. During the California gold rush — actually, just about every gold rush in history — people seemed to lose their minds at the thought of attaining a little wealth. They abandoned logic and reason (as well as their jobs and families) in hopes of getting rich, and did everything from claim jumping to murder in order to get what they wanted. What would they do if the nigh-limitless power of an Incarnate was dangled in front of them?

"Okay," I said. "I get it. People will do almost anything for wealth and power, and if they knew how to become an Incarnate, you'd have billions clawing each other's eyes out for the chance."

"Pretty much," Rune admitted, "which is why we don't tell people how to become one."

# INCARNATION

"But you also said that an Incarnate can 'arise.' That implies that it's something that can happen" — I spent a moment searching for the right word — "what, naturally?"

"Something like that. Occasionally a new force or power comes into being, and some person becomes the physical manifestation of it — an Incarnate."

I spent a moment letting his words roll around in my brain. Rune, watching me ponder and clearly wanting me to fully grasp the concept, took the opportunity to help me out with an example.

"Think about when mankind first split the atom," he said. "All of a sudden you had nuclear power — this new force that hadn't existed before. And then, in very short order, you had to appoint a department or person to be in charge of it, control it, oversee it, etcetera. Likewise, some new *puissance* might herald the advent of a new Incarnate."

I nodded. "All right, that puts it in terms I can grasp a little easier."

"Great," Rune said. "But I think all this talk of how someone becomes an Incarnate is getting us sidetracked."

I gave him an incredulous look. "You don't think that how a person becomes an Incarnate might have a bearing on how he can be killed?"

He seemed to dwell on the question for a moment, and then stated, "Fair enough. More importantly, your observation highlights why we need your help."

I raised an eyebrow. "Oh? How so?"

"Frankly speaking, we have terrible detective skills."

I laughed. "I would think that, with the power Incarnates wield, you people would be the best detectives in the universe." I put my forefingers and thumbs together, then spread them out like a banner unfurling as I pretended to read a headline, stating, "Rune the Incarnate, Private Eye. No Crime Unsolved."

"Hilarious," Rune deadpanned. "In truth, however, you're not that far off-base. Under most circumstances, if an Incarnate wanted to know what had happened in a particular instance, we could just read the minds of those involved, go back in time and look at the incident, or something else along those lines. We've basically never needed to be good at being gumshoes, because determining the truth in any particular scenario has never been problematic."

"So, what's the problem with doing any of that stuff now?" I asked. "Reading minds, for instance."

"For one thing, it's impossible to read the mind of an Incarnate unless they allow it," Rune replied. "And even if they do, you can't be sure that what they're allowing you to observe is what really happened."

I nodded as this information sank in. From past experience with Rune, I knew that Incarnates could warp reality. That being the case, they could create fake memories without breaking a sweat.

"So, in essence, you read each other's minds and everyone had an alibi."

"Uh…" Rune droned. "Not exactly."

I gave him a look that I was sure conveyed my bewilderment, but before I could ask him to explain himself, Rune sat up and cocked his head to the side.

"Let's finish this later," he said, getting to his feet. "We have company."

Following my companion's lead, I stood up and turned to the doors, which were just starting to open, and

# INCARNATION

in walked a man who — much to my surprise — was as much a spectacle as Rune.

# INCARNATION

## Chapter 5

The man who entered our suite appeared to be young — maybe in his mid-twenties — with long brown hair that was braided and hung down his back. Maybe an inch shorter than my six-foot height, he had comely features and an easygoing smile. However, that was where anything close to "normal" in terms of appearance ended.

For starters, the newcomer — from head to foot — seemed to be covered in water. That's not to say that he was soaked, like someone who'd gotten caught in a rainstorm without an umbrella (although to a certain extent that appeared to be the case). It was more the fact that water seemed to run all over his body, starting at the crown of his head and cascading down, with small undulations flowing across his skin, like ripples on a fountain wall.

In addition, even his clothes appeared to be made of water. Or rather, to be more exact, I garnered the impression that he was clothed *with* water. From his shoulders to his ankles, he was seemingly "dressed" in liquid that approximated the shape of a full-length overcoat (and which was also, thankfully, murky and therefore visually impenetrable to the naked eye). The surface of his attire appeared to roil with small breakers and swells that would surge and crest frothily on a continual basis. Taken altogether, it was if he had somehow managed to drape himself in a miniature ocean.

Finally, as one might expect, water naturally pooled beneath him as he walked. (And I noticed that, like his clothes, he wore sandals that appeared to be made of water as well.) However, rather than leave a trail like someone traipsing through a house after coming inside from a downpour, the liquid followed him around, almost like it were his shadow, leaving the floor dry in its wake.

Without being told, I inherently sensed that our visitor was an Incarnate. Smiling, he walked toward my companion.

"Rune," the man said in greeting.

At the same time, something like a deluge came out of nowhere, soaking Rune to the skin. It was as if someone had held an invisible bucket of water over his head and then dumped it on him. (Oddly enough, nothing besides Rune got wet.)

"Really, Mariner?" Rune muttered as the new arrival — Mariner — laughed heartily.

"In case you forgot, I owed you from last time," Mariner said with a grin. "Now we're even."

Mariner made a gesture with his hand, and Rune was immediately dry again, all traces of water gone as if they'd never existed.

"Better?" Mariner asked.

"I suppose," Rune answered. "Although I would have been just as happy never to have been wet at all."

Ignoring him, Mariner glanced at me, then back at my companion. "Well, aren't you going to introduce me?"

"Sure," Rune replied. "Jim, this is Mariner. Mariner, Jim."

Mariner extended a hand in my direction and I instinctively reached for it, momentarily forgetting that he was literally covered with water. As a result, I expected a cold and clammy handshake. Much to my surprise, the hand I shook was dry, with the liquid covering him having apparently receded just before we made contact.

I looked him in the eye as we shook hands and exchanged pleasantries, and noticed something that took me almost completely by surprise. The water flowing down from his crown didn't just cascade across his skin, like his forehead, brow, and eyelids. It actually ran over his eyeballs, as well — something that I initially found unsettling.

However, if I reacted out of the ordinary in any way, Mariner didn't seem to notice. He released my hand and took a seat at the end of the couch, which immediately became soaked. I took a seat at the opposite end, thankful that the water clinging to our guest didn't spread far enough across to reach me. Rune, following suit, sat back down in the chair he'd previously occupied.

"Well, they told me you had a *laamuffal*," Mariner began, glancing at me, "so I just had to see for myself."

I frowned upon hearing that weird term obviously applied to me again, but didn't say anything.

"And your task?" Mariner continued.

Rune simply gestured toward me, causing our visitor to look in my direction again, although this time his gaze lingered a little longer.

"Seems young," Mariner noted after a few seconds, "although I do sense aptitude."

"It was short notice," Rune declared. "I had to work with what was available."

"Perhaps he could speak with Sayo while we converse?" Mariner suggested. As he spoke, he hooked a thumb over his shoulder, and for the first time I realized that there was a fourth person in the room. (Apparently I had been so preoccupied with Mariner's unique appearance that I hadn't even noticed.)

It was a young woman whom I judged to be just a few years older than me — maybe nineteen or twenty — and dressed in what seemed to be a cheongsam coat with a pair of leggings underneath. Like Mariner, she had her hair braided (although hers was done in triplicate, with three braids hanging down on each side of her head).

The young woman, Sayo (who was standing a few feet behind Mariner), turned to me and gave a slight bow of her head. I glanced at Rune, who gave me a subtle nod. Taking that as my cue, I stood up and walked toward her.

"Hi," I said, extending my hand. "I'm Jim."

She reached out and took my hand, firmly shaking it once while at the same time executing a slight bow. "A pleasure to meet you, Jim. I'm Sayo. Shall we retire to your quarters?"

My eyebrows shot up in surprise. "My quarters?"

"Yes," she replied. "The Incarnates wish to speak privately, and the Inscrutable's chambers" — she gestured toward the door leading to Rune's quarters — "are clearly off-limits. That leaves your room."

I frowned at her use of the term "inscrutable," not quite knowing what to make of it. However, before I could question her about it, she turned and began walking toward the door Rune had identified as being the entrance to my quarters.

# INCARNATION

## Chapter 6

The space Rune had designated for my personal use turned out to be on par with a large, one-bedroom apartment. Upon entering with Sayo, I closed the door behind us, and then took a quick look around.

The place opened up into a cozy sitting room that was seemingly the center of the apartment. From there, I could make out a kitchen and dining area, and through an open door set off to the side I could see the foot of a bed, marking that area as the bedroom.

Without waiting for an invitation, Sayo took a seat in a nearby lounge chair. I sat down at the end of a love seat diagonal to her.

"So, you are Rune's *laamuffal*," she said.

I shrugged. "I don't know. I'm not sure what that word even means."

"Then allow me to explain," Sayo stated, beaming. "A *laamuffal* assists an Incarnate in any way possible, whether that be obtaining items for his use, carrying out his orders, or simply making sure the Incarnate is at all times comfortable."

"Kind of like a servant," I surmised with a frown.

She nodded. "Serving a *Chomarsus* is a privilege, and I feel honored to be a *laamuffal*, just as you should be honored to serve Rune in that same capacity."

At that moment, I had my own thoughts about being Rune's servant, but it was nothing that could be said in polite society. Deciding to table the *laamuffal* topic for the moment, I instead changed the subject.

"What do you know about the Incarnate who was killed?" I asked.

She gave me an inquisitive look. "You mean Gamma?"

"Uh...I don't know," I admitted. "I don't think anyone's told me her name. I just know she was murdered."

"Then yes, you're referring to Gamma," Sayo confirmed. "As to your question, I knew her by virtue of my role as Mariner's *laamuffal*, but we didn't socialize."

"What was she like?"

Sayo gave me a blank stare. "She was an Incarnate," she said flatly after a moment, as if that explained everything.

"But what was she *like*?" I asked again. "Mean? Nice? Friendly? Aloof? What?"

Sayo looked down. "It's not for me to comment on the disposition of a *Chomarsus*."

*Great*, I thought. *She reveres Incarnates so much that she can't —*

"However," Sayo continued, catching me off guard, "I found her to be" — she hesitated for a moment, as if searching for the proper word — "pleasant. Congenial. I liked her. Her death is a real blow."

Reaching out empathically, I picked up on feelings of sadness and melancholy. Sayo's grief, while not overwhelming, was definitely real.

"I'm sorry," I said, reaching out to give her a sympathetic pat on the hand. "Any idea how she died?"

She shook her head. "No one knows."

"So I've heard," I acknowledged. "But there have to be rumors or speculation."

"The only thing anyone is certain of is that another Incarnate must have done it," she stated, then gave me an odd look. "Why are you so interested in this subject?"

My first instinct was to sidestep the question, but then it occurred to me that she'd find out soon enough.

"It's why I'm here," I stated. "To find out who killed her."

Sayo's face suddenly took on a slightly nervous expression. At the same time, I felt a slight twinge of anxiety emanating from her.

"Well," she said, coming to her feet, "we should be getting back."

"Ah, sure," I muttered, standing as well.

Sayo started heading for the door, with me right on her heels. Moments later, we were back in the main living room.

Seeing us approach, Mariner and Rune appeared to wrap up their conversation, with the former rising from the couch. Much to my surprise, I noticed that when he vacated his seat, the moisture seemingly left with him. Rather than having a large wet spot on it where Mariner had been seated, the couch appeared to be as dry as it had been before he sat.

"Please keep me posted," Mariner said to Rune, who simply nodded. Seemingly satisfied, Mariner turned to me.

"Nice meeting you, Jim," he said. "Hopefully you won't find the job of being Rune's *laamuffal* too onerous."

A moment later, he and Sayo simply vanished, leaving no evidence — not even a drop of water — that they'd ever been present.

# INCARNATION

## Chapter 7

"There's that word again," I said after our two visitors were gone. "*Laamuffal.* You'll be happy to know that I've found out what it means, no thanks to you."

Rune's eyebrows rose momentarily in surprise, and then I saw understanding dawn in his eyes.

"Sayo," he muttered.

"Yeah," I stated with a nod.

"So what did she say?"

"Enough for me to figure out that a *laamuffal* is basically a sycophant."

"Whoa," he grumbled. "That's kind of harsh, don't you think?"

"No," I replied, shaking my head adamantly. "Harsh is your fellow Incarnate brainwashing a young girl into thinking that waiting on him hand and foot is her divine purpose."

"She's not young," Rune shot back.

"What?" I blurted out, not sure what he was talking about.

"Sayo," he clarified. "She was born in Japan over two thousand years ago, contrary to your theory about being young and brainwashed."

"So he took her from a time period and culture where women were already subservient," I noted. "In essence, he didn't have to do any brainwashing. Society had already done it for him."

Rune seem to bristle at this. "Well, while you're up on your high horse, you might want to consider the fact that serving an Incarnate has resulted in her being gifted with an incredibly long life, as well as seeing wonders that most people have never even imagined."

"Oh, so instead of living only a single lifetime of indentured servitude — say, fifty years — she should be turning cartwheels that she got to serve for forty of them?"

"What is this, some new superpower you've developed?" Rune practically demanded. "The ability to twist pros into cons, and recast positive attributes as negative traits? Because I swear, it was *not* on your résumé."

We stared at each other for a moment — and then both burst out laughing. Although the conversation had seemed to be getting heated, it was pretty clear that neither of us was taking it too seriously.

"Look," Rune said, after taking a few moments to compose himself. "I appreciate what you're saying, but I brought you here to be Sherlock Holmes, not Susan B. Anthony. So put away the suffrage bonnet and put on your detective hat."

"Fine," I said. "By the way, here's a question that's been bugging me: why me?"

Rune's brow furrowed. "Why you what?"

"How'd you settle on me to help you with this? I mean, I can follow the logic of you guys needing a hand because — due to your powers — you don't think the right way for detective work. But why not just scoop up a *real* detective for this stuff — some cop who's been working homicide for twenty years and has well-honed instincts about murder and suspects? Or better yet, why not someone like Mouse?"

At the thought of him, I reflected on the fact that Mouse would probably be perfect for this. He was not only the leader of the Alpha League (as well as my League-assigned mentor), but he was quite possibly the smartest man who ever lived. He'd probably have solved Gamma's murder in an hour.

# INCARNATION

"It would take a regular detective forever just to get up to speed on the concept of Incarnates, let alone things like this place being outside of space and time — assuming he could wrap his mind around them. You, on the other hand, already had basic knowledge about Incarnates, you've been to places like this before, and—"

"*A* place," I interjected. "I've been to *a* place like this before."

"Still, that's more than most others can say."

"So I've got the requisite background and experience," I summed up.

"Yes," he said with a nod. "In addition, we're dealing with a murderous Incarnate. Thus, even if we rounded up an experienced detective, there would be concern about his welfare."

"You mean that the guilty party might kill him if he started getting too close."

"In a nutshell."

"But you people are Incarnates," I stressed. "Wouldn't you be able to protect him?"

"Did you forget that one of us has been killed?" he asked. "Apparently we can't even protect ourselves."

"So you need someone with powers," I deduced.

"We *prefer* someone with powers," he corrected.

"Does that even matter?" I asked. "Is having powers going to protect them from a killer Incarnate?"

"Probably not," Rune admitted. "But we'd like to think we're not just setting up a turkey shoot."

"Is that why you struck Mouse off the list?" I asked. "Because he lacks superpowers?"

"Ha!" Rune bellowed, letting out a bark of laughter. "Mouse *has* powers, and they make him formidable. However, he's busy with another issue."

# INCARNATION

His statement caused me to raise an eyebrow. Mouse and I had just finished dealing with a matter involving a clone of me shortly before I'd allowed Rune to whisk me away. I found it bothersome that another problem had seemingly landed on his doorstep almost immediately — then almost laughed at the irony, considering that the same thing had essentially happened to me. (I shelved for later discussion the comment about Mouse's powers, although it was the most intriguing thing Rune had said due to the fact that I'd never seen Mouse exhibit any abilities I'd define as "super.")

"Okay," I said, "even with Mouse off your short list, why not go with a full-fledged member of the Alpha League instead of someone like me, who's just a part of the teen affiliate? Alpha Prime, for instance."

Rune shook his head. "He may be the most powerful superhero on Earth and generally a good guy, but your old man's not right for this."

I fought hard to hide my surprise. Although Alpha Prime was — as Rune stated — widely hailed as the most powerful super on the planet, not many people knew he was my father. I was tempted to ask Rune how *he* knew, but decided to hold my tongue.

"Basically," he went on, "the issue with using Alpha Prime in this instance — just about any League member, in fact — is that it presents the same problem as having us Incarnates investigate: lack of the proper skills."

I pondered on this for a moment, and then the answer came to me.

"Mouse," I said flatly.

"Bingo," Rune uttered with a nod. "That guy has been the brains of the League for the past few years — the researcher, the battle tactician, the investigator, the problem-solver…"

"So what are you saying?" I asked. "That the rest of the League's gone stupid?"

"No," he said, laughing. "Far from it. I'm just saying that, on the whole, their problem-solving skills have gone to pot. You, on the other hand, have displayed an innate ability to solve mysteries, as well as a talent for thinking on your feet — not to mention the fact that you've got a wide array of superpowers."

"Which still may not be enough to keep me from getting killed," I added sarcastically.

"Hmmm," Rune mumbled. "Apparently I need to add 'pessimist' to your list of attributes."

# INCARNATION

## Chapter 8

We left our suite a few minutes after Rune finished explaining to me why I was the right man to investigate Gamma's death. Personally, I wasn't convinced, but I was willing to give it the old college try.

"Where are we going?" I asked as we walked through a wide castle hallway.

"The Cosmos Corridor," he answered. "And before you ask, it's easier to show it to you than explain it."

"That's fine," I replied. "Any reason we're trudging through the castle instead of you just taking us there?"

Rune cast a quick glance in my direction. "You're thinking about Mariner — the way he and Sayo left our suite."

"Yeah," I admitted with a nod. "Seems like you Incarnates would dispense with the drudgery of parading around on foot most of the time."

"Wow," Rune practically lamented. "You must view Incarnates as incredibly lazy."

"Not lazy," I protested. "I just assumed you'd do what was most efficient."

My companion shook his head solemnly. "You ever heard the expression, 'the journey is part of the destination'?"

"I think so — or at least something like it. It sort of means that if you focus only on the destination, you miss out on things along the way."

"Well, that essentially sums up my feelings on the subject," he intoned. "Besides, the Cosmos Corridor falls under the purview of another Incarnate, so just appearing out of thin air would be rude."

# INCARNATION

"I take it that's why Mariner came through the front door when he arrived at our suite."

"Correct," Rune said with a nod. "Leaving, on the other hand, is kind of left to your discretion."

"So that means we'll just be disappearing when we depart someone's company?"

"Maybe," Rune admitted. "And that reminds me: much of what you see around here and witness Incarnates do is going to be thaumaturgy. The magical and mystical run rampant here, so not everything will be logical. However, there won't be a bunch of chants, incantations, and stuff like that. It'll just happen."

"Wait a minute," I protested. "I've seen you do incantations before."

"Theatrics. If you're a magician, people expect and want a show, so sometimes I give it to them."

"Well, in case you didn't know, I'm not well-versed in spells, enchantments, and stuff. Maybe you should have recruited a wizard to help you instead."

"Nah," Rune stressed, shaking his head. "We're in good hands with you."

\*\*\*\*\*\*\*\*\*\*\*\*\*\*\*\*\*\*\*\*\*\*\*\*\*\*\*\*\*\*\*\*\*\*\*\*\*\*

We spent the next few minutes walking in relative silence, finally coming to a halt in front of a black door that had a field of stars painted on it. A moment later, I found myself doing a double take as I realized something unusual about the door: the stars on it were twinkling. Seconds later, something like a comet shot across the field of view being shown. It suddenly dawned on me that the door wasn't painted, but somehow represented a "live" view of some region of outer space.

# INCARNATION

Incredulous, I turned toward Rune and found him grinning broadly.

"I know — it's a lot to take in when you first see it," he said, plainly amused by my surprise. "Come on."

With that, he stepped through the door — literally. Basically, he didn't bother opening it; instead, he just stepped into the field of stars and vanished.

Still recovering from my amazement regarding the image on the door, I quickly followed Rune's lead and walked through the door.

# INCARNATION

## Chapter 9

We found ourselves in a room that, to be frank, really appeared to be a continuation of the door. We were completely enveloped by darkness, punctuated by a random scattering of small, glimmering lights — stars. They were all around us: above, beside, below. Moreover, they seemed to extend infinitely in all directions, even beneath our feet. (Which brought to mind another question: what the heck were we standing on?)

Using the term "we" however, was a bit of a misnomer, as I couldn't see anything other than the stars around me. That said, I could sense someone empathically, although I immediately realized that it wasn't Rune. Remembering that there was a murderer on the loose, I quickly — almost in a panic — cycled my vision through the light spectrum until I could see somewhat akin to normally.

Rune, as expected, was a few feet away from me. Also nearby was the source of the emotions I'd felt — a young woman.

She was about five-foot-eight, attractive, and seemed to be in her early twenties (although apparent age around here obviously meant nothing). Her hair, short and dark, was worn in a layered style that appeared messy but actually framed her face in an appealing way. Finally, she wore something like a jumpsuit that shimmered slightly, although not as brightly as the stars around us.

"The Inscrutable Rune," she uttered with a smile, heading toward my companion.

"Ursula," he said, stepping forward and giving the woman a quick hug.

"Who's your friend?" Ursula asked, gesturing toward me. "He's cute."

She followed up her comment with a wink and a smile, making me blush.

"This is Jim," Rune said. "Jim, say hello to Ursula."

I stepped forward and extended my hand, saying, "Nice to meet you."

"Bump that," Ursula declared, playfully smacking my hand away. "I'm a hugger."

With that, she stepped in close and gave me a firm embrace that probably straddled the line between platonic and something more. Caught flat-footed, I returned the gesture by putting my hands delicately on her shoulders.

After a few seconds, Ursula stepped back and eyed me critically.

"Your hugs are pathetic," she declared. "We're going to work on that."

Unsure of how to respond, I reached out empathically and picked up on feelings of kindness and affability, as well as a highly sociable demeanor — but nothing overtly romantic. A moment later, the truth hit me, and I almost laughed: Ursula was just a big flirt.

"I look forward to it," I said to her with a grin. "I could use the practice."

She smiled back, and appeared to be on the verge of making an additional comment when Rune spoke up.

"So," he droned, getting Ursula's attention. "Is she around?"

Ursula nodded. "Yes. She stepped out for a moment, but should be back momentarily." Without warning, Ursula then tilted her head to the side, as if listening for something. "In fact, right…about…*now*."

# INCARNATION

Perfectly in sync with Ursula's verbal cue, a woman appeared in the room, essentially out of nowhere. I found myself staring at her intently. She was the most alluring woman I'd ever seen.

# INCARNATION

## Chapter 10

She was tall — at least my height, and maybe an inch or so taller (which would have put her at six-one). Her large, doe-like eyes were a mesmerizing violet in color, framed by long, thick lashes and punctuated by immaculately-manicured eyebrows. She had lips that were full and pouty, along with a flawless complexion that was bronze in color. In addition, she had a perfectly-proportioned hourglass figure, on which she currently sported a form-fitting, one-piece bodysuit.

As I continued looking her over, I kept finding more complimentary features: a too-cute nose, a graceful neckline, etcetera. Truth be told, the list of her attributes went on endlessly. It was as though every textbook indicator of feminine beauty and allure — from large eyes to glowing skin to long legs — had been wondrously combined into a single package. Her most striking feature, however, was the fact that she was completely and absolutely bald, without a single strand of hair on her head. Oddly enough, the lack thereof only made her that much more fascinating.

"Hey, you want to put your eyes back in your head?"

I blinked, snapping out of my reverie as I realized that Rune had just spoken to me.

"Huh?" I murmured, trying to get my thoughts organized.

"You're practically drooling," Rune chided.

The woman who had just appeared laughed, her mirth sounding absolutely melodic.

"Leave him alone, Rune," she said, smiling as she walked toward us. "He's not hurting anyone."

# INCARNATION

Rune let out an annoyed groan in response, but didn't say anything. A moment later, the new arrival stopped in front of us, then leaned forward to give my companion a hug, which he returned. A moment later, she stepped back and turned in my direction. After taking a quick glance at me, she looked back at Rune expectantly.

"Oh, sorry," Rune muttered a few seconds later. Having realized what was expected of him, he quickly made introductions, giving the woman's name as Endow.

"Endow is the leader of the Incarnates," he explained.

"Not true," Endow protested. "We don't have a leader."

"First among equals, then," Rune countered, which Endow didn't protest.

Looking at Rune, she then gestured toward me. "So, this is the one?" she asked.

Rune merely nodded in return.

"Well, let's assess," Endow said.

Now it was apparently the woman's turn to look *me* over, because she suddenly gave me a piercing stare. However, what she did was a lot more than simply gazing. Her eyes began to sparkle, and I felt them boring into me, seeing things that weren't just on the surface, but embedded deep within — things that were an intricate part of me.

After about thirty seconds (although it felt much longer), the sparkle in her eyes diminished. A moment later, she looked away with a pensive expression on her face.

"Hmmm," she droned, then turned to Rune. "He's not one of mine."

"I didn't say he was," Rune shot back.

"Wait a minute," I interjected. "One of your what?"

No one immediately answered. Instead, while Ursula stood off to the side, Rune and Endow exchanged a knowing look.

"Shall we show him?" Endow asked a moment later.

Rune gave an indifferent shrug.

Taking that as an affirmative, Endow began glancing around the room excitedly, as if she was looking for something. All of a sudden, her gaze seem to settle on one area. She pointed a finger, and that part of the room seemed to rush toward us. Or rather, one of the stars situated there came racing in our direction, expanding as it got closer. It stopped about a dozen paces from us, at which point the star had ballooned to the size of a basketball and sat there floating at about the height of my chest.

As I watched it, I quickly realized that it wasn't just a star that was floating before us; it was an entire solar system. I spent a few moments staring in awe as I watched various worlds spinning on their axes while following their orbits around this particular sun.

I leaned toward Ursula and whispered, "Is this real?"

"You better believe it," she whispered back while softly snickering (presumably at my ignorance).

Endow pointed at one of the planets circling the star — a blue-green bauble that looked fairly familiar; it immediately expanded while the rest of its solar system receded in size. Endow made a circular motion with her hand, and it was as if a camera lens began zooming in on the planet, passing first through the upper atmosphere, and then a cloud layer before homing in on one of the land masses.

The "camera" kept diving down, ultimately focusing on a mountainous region that ran parallel to an eye-catching shoreline. Winding its way through the mountains was a narrow, twisting road, and as I looked, I noticed a small red dot zipping along the thoroughfare in question. It didn't take much imagination to understand what I was seeing, and my suspicions were proven correct moments later when the image magnified, revealing a red convertible sportscar with some thirty-something guy behind the wheel. He was wearing sunglasses and had the top down (of course), and was obviously driving well in excess of the posted speed limit.

It wasn't clear what happened, but all of a sudden, the driver lost control of the vehicle. One second, he was cruising along, trying to set a new land speed record; the next, he was fighting to keep the car on the road as the vehicle fishtailed all over the place. And then the car smashed through the guardrail and went sailing over the side of the mountain.

The view then froze on an image of the driver, mouth open and looking completely terrified. More to the point, I could actually feel his dread empathically.

"Ursula," Endow said, without taking her eyes off the driver.

By this time, I had already discerned that Ursula was Endow's *laamuffal*, and this became fully evident when — upon hearing her name — Ursula immediately went into motion. She walked swiftly to one side of the room and seemed to bend down and grab what I initially took to be a bundle of stars. A moment later, I realized that it was some type of square-shaped receptacle, camouflaged in such a way as to appear almost indistinguishable from the actual stars around us.

With the container in hand, Ursula hustled back to Endow, who gently took it from her. She then lifted the top part of the receptacle (which turned out to be a hinged lid), revealing several rows of what looked like glowing, colored gems inside. Endow spent a moment staring at the gems, each of which was about the size of my thumbnail, and then — after selecting a blue one — she closed the lid and handed the container back to Ursula.

While her *laamuffal* went to put the receptacle back, Endow turned to the still-frozen image of the sportscar driver and placed the blue gemstone on his forehead. The stone flashed for a moment and then seemed to vanish. A moment later, the scene came to life again, with the driver wailing like a banshee as his car plunged toward the ground.

Like some car-chase movie, the vehicle didn't simply nosedive and smash into the ground at the bottom of the mountain. Instead, it bounced along, turning cartwheels and going into barrel rolls and such as it struck peaks, crags, and outcroppings of rock on its way down. Eventually, however, it did reach the foot of the mountain where, battered, mangled, and leaking fuel, it finally came to a halt upside down.

Based on what had been observed visually, one would have thought that the driver had to be dead. However, my empathic senses were telling me something different. A few seconds later, as I anticipated, the driver came crawling out from under the wreck that had been his car, looking like an absolute mess and exuding shock at the fact that he was not only alive, but completely uninjured.

# INCARNATION

At that juncture, Endow made the circular motion with her hand again and the entire scene vanished. She then turned to me, smiling.

"You saved him," I said, succinctly summing up what we'd just seen.

"Actually, I did a little more than that," she asserted. "He has a destiny to fulfill which requires certain unique talents, so I made him invulnerable."

My eyes went up in surprise. "Excuse me?"

"She made him a super," Rune explained.

I frowned, focusing on previous comments that were now starting to make sense.

"Wait a minute," I intoned. "She gave him powers?"

"Yes," Rune confirmed with a nod. "It's one of the things she does. She gifts people with certain abilities."

I looked at Endow. "So when you said earlier that I wasn't one of yours…"

"I was saying that you didn't get your powers from me," she clarified.

"Okay, I get that," I stressed. "But the statement implies that *someone* gave me my powers. Is that what you're saying?"

"No, not at all," Endow assured me. "When Rune first told me about you, I was surprised. You possess an exceptionally rare combination of powers and abilities, but to have them all manifest naturally is rarer still. I thought that perhaps you had been gifted with some while others developed on their own, but from what I can see that isn't the case. All of your talents are undoubtedly innate."

I let out a sigh of relief. For some reason, it bothered me immensely that my powers might have come by virtue of someone like Endow. Not that she seemed like a bad person; it was simply the fact that my powers were an essential part of who I was, and the notion that I might be beholden to someone for them bothered me.

"So where are you from, Jim?" said a feminine voice, interrupting my thoughts.

It was Ursula. Glancing around, I suddenly realized that while I had been reflecting on my powers, Rune and Endow had moved on to another subject. Apparently thinking that I hadn't heard her, Ursula repeated her question.

"Um…Earth," I replied.

"I know that, dingbat," she uttered playfully. "I meant *where* on Earth."

"Oh," I muttered, my head still not quite in the conversation. "Uh…"

"Never mind," she said, shaking her head dismissively. Then she perked up slightly and said, "You wanna see something really cool?"

# INCARNATION

## Chapter 11

I had to admit to being impressed. It appeared that Ursula, like Endow, also had the ability to manipulate items in the room, and — after dragging me to a far side of the room away from the two Incarnates — she brought to the fore a number of items that were completely fascinating to observe: black holes, quasars, supernovas...

"So," I said after Ursula just finished showing me a pulsar, "how far can you reach from here?"

She considered the question for a moment. "You mean how far into space or into time?"

"Uh..." I muttered, not really having thought about the question in those terms. "Both, I guess."

"Everywhere. Every*when*. All space, all time. The entire universe."

"So you can reach out to any time and place, and observe what's happening," I summed up.

She nodded. "Generally, yes."

A canorous laugh rang out unexpectedly, and I glanced over to where Endow, giggling merrily, was still speaking to Rune.

"Hmmm," I muttered, reflecting on Ursula's answer as I turned back to her. "Why do you say 'generally'?"

"Well, the Cosmos Corridor is the only place in Permovren where it's possible. Of course, you can't see other places like this that are outside of space and time – and you can't observe or affect Incarnates – but otherwise the sky's the limit."

"And if you decide you want to give someone an ability — say, super speed — you can just do it?"

"Well, *I* can't," she admitted, laughing. "That falls under the province of Endow."

"Impressive," I noted, and found myself glancing once again in Endow's direction as I reflected on the power — the *sivrrut* — she wielded.

"Hey!" Ursula snapped, getting my attention. "You're not going to last long as my new beau if you keep ogling other women. You don't want to end up like my last boyfriend."

Grinning, I raised an eyebrow. "What happened to him?"

"I dropped him into a black hole over there," she said, pointing to a far section of the room. Then she spun and pointed to a different area, muttering, "Or did I strand him on a desert planet over there? Or…"

Biting her lip, she trailed off as she appeared to ponder on something. A moment later, she flung up her hands in capitulation, saying, "I don't know. I can't keep up with all these dudes."

At this point, I was laughing heartily, having decided that I liked Ursula and her sense of humor. A moment later, she joined me, snickering.

It took a few moments for our laughter to subside, at which point, still chuckling, I said, "Well, I appreciate the heads-up, but I don't think you'd find me good boyfriend material. I'm a little on the young side."

"Hold up," she said, sobering instantly. "How old do you think I am?"

I shrugged. "Twenty-four, twenty-five?"

"I'm seventeen," she declared defensively, putting her hands on her hips and glowering at me.

I stared at her, plainly surprised. "Seventeen *hundred?*"

She looked at me incredulously, then firmly stated, "No! Just seventeen, as in one-seven."

"Uh, sorry," I mumbled. "You look very mature for your age. I apologize if I offended you."

She continued glaring at me, then winked and smiled.

"Just kidding," she said. "About being mad, that is — not about being seventeen."

"Really?" I asked.

She nodded. "Yeah. Despite being *laamuffal* to an Incarnate, I just felt like I wasn't taken as seriously when I looked like a teenager, so I had Endow age me a few years."

"She can do that?" I queried in surprise.

"Of course. All the Incarnates can. Traditionally, the *laamuffal* gets to select their own appearance, which makes sense when you consider that you might be on the job for a *long* time."

I nodded, reflecting back on my conversation with Rune about Sayo. At the time, it hadn't even occurred to me to ask about her youthful appearance, but now I understood.

"Anyway," Ursula said, interrupting my thoughts, "I've been showing you all the stuff *I* find interesting. What's something *you'd* like to see?"

"Huh?" I muttered, not sure I understood the question.

She made a gesture that encompassed the room. "We've got the entire universe here. Surely there's something you're interested in taking a peek at?"

"I don't know," I said. "Obviously, I haven't really thought about it."

"Well, give me something to work with," Ursula insisted. "Maybe there's a distant planet you're interested in, or a far-off galaxy. Or maybe just see what people are saying when you aren't in the room."

"I'm a telepath," I blurted out, although my powers were actually limited in that regard. "I've occasionally picked up on thoughts that people have about me that I'm sure they believed were private, and it's not always pretty. Hearing what they say about me when I'm not around is something I am definitely *not* interested in."

As I spoke, I found my conviction on the subject solidifying. Watching people talk about me when I wasn't around was completely off the table.

"Are you sure?" Ursula asked. "Maybe see if your grandparents brag about you to their friends? See how your mom really felt about that bowl you made her in kindergarten? Check in on your ex and see if she's missing you?"

Despite my sentiments on the subject, Ursula's last question actually piqued my interest. (My girlfriend had just broken up with me, but it was something I was trying not to dwell on.) More to the point, I must have telegraphed that fact in some way because it didn't go unnoticed.

"A-ha!" Ursula crowed. "The ex. It's always the ex."

"Not this time," I countered. "I'm not interested. There's nothing I want to see."

"Are you sure?" she implored.

"Nothing comes to mind."

She seemed to reflect on that for a moment.

"Okay, maybe *consciously* you don't want to see anything," she conceded, "but perhaps *sub*consciously?"

I stared at her, nonplussed. "What do you mean?"

Rather than respond, Ursula lifted her hands in front of her. Her eyes narrowed, and she began swiftly running her thumbs across the fingers on each respective hand, similar to someone making a gesture for cash. Almost immediately, a soft amber glow formed around her fingertips.

"Close your eyes," she said.

I was a little unsure of what was happening, but based on what I could sense of her emotions, I felt I could trust Ursula. That being the case, I complied, and a moment later I felt her fingers on my temples.

"Clear your mind," she said. "Try not to think of anything. Just focus on my voice. Now think about Christmas."

I frowned, wondering where this was going.

"*Focus*," Ursula practically commanded, letting me know my facial expression hadn't gone unnoticed.

Somewhat chagrinned, I redoubled my efforts at cooperating.

"Christmas," she said again. "Think about Christmas."

I let my mind flit through things about the holiday in question: the lights. Decorations. Nativity. Christmas cheer. Presents.

"Good," Ursula muttered in an encouraging tone. "Now think about the best Christmas you ever had. Everything that was on your list to Santa, all the wonderful gifts you got. Excellent... Now think about your birthday — your *best* birthday. The birthday that you remember more fondly than all the others. Think of the best gift you got that day. Great — you're doing great. Now focus on what you got to observe in here today. Think about the wonders of the universe that you laid eyes on. Black holes. Quasars. A gorgeous *laamuffal* who should be gracing magazine covers."

# INCARNATION

I fought to keep from cracking up after her last comment, and I picked up on Ursùla's mirth as well.

"Okay," she said as she took her hands from my temple. "You can open your eyes now."

I did as she asked, and then stared at what was in front of me.

# INCARNATION

## Chapter 12

Before us was an image that primarily consisted of a long beam of bluish-white light about three inches in width. It appeared to stretch between two worlds that looked amazingly similar. (In fact, with the beam of light connecting them, the two planets looked remarkably similar to a set of vintage globe barbells.)

However, it wasn't so much the imagery that stunned me, but more so the fact that I was sensing things on an empathic level. Leaning in closely, I saw what appeared to be two man-shaped figures within the beam of light. They were the source of the emotions I was picking up on. Their features were obscured by the beam's light, but I didn't need to see them in further detail. Empathically, I was familiar with the pair. I knew who they were.

Caught completely by surprise, I started laughing.

Ursula smiled at me. "I take it this is familiar to you."

"Yes," I confirmed with a nod. "I knew a couple of guys who went through some kind of dimensional vortex." I pointed at the two man-shaped figures in the beam of light. "Apparently, this is them."

Ursula stared at the scene for a moment, then turned to me. "Friends of yours?"

"Something like that."

She didn't say anything, choosing instead to simply nod, her brow now crinkled.

"How'd you do this?" I asked.

My question seemed to bring Ursula back to herself, as her usual smile quickly moved back into place.

"It wasn't that hard," she insisted. "Ask people to think about Christmas, and their thoughts invariably turn to presents. They'll think about what they received as gifts — and subconsciously they'll reflect on what they wanted but *didn't* get. Same with birthdays: they'll consciously ruminate on what they got, and subconsciously focus on the item they wish they'd been given. So when I asked you about the things you saw in here, you consciously mulled over what you were shown—"

"But subconsciously I mused on something I wanted to see," I interjected.

"Is it what you expected?" she asked.

"Honestly, I've never thought too much about it," I asserted, which was true. "At least not consciously."

We both laughed at that, and then I added, "Seriously, thanks for showing me this."

"No problem," she assured me. "As I said, there's always something, although I really did think it was going to be the ex."

I frowned as I considered her words. "So, since you pulled this out of my head, does that mean you're a telepath?"

"Not really," she confessed, shaking her head. "Typically, if I'm initiating it, I have to have contact with the person, and I need them to sort of lead me where I need to go — the way I had to talk you into letting me see things. I can't just dive into their heads and start digging up info. However, if the other person is a telepath and they open the mental door, so to speak, I'm not as restrained."

I nodded, completely understanding, as Ursula's telepathic limitations mimicked my own to a certain extent.

"But since we're on the subject of abilities," she said, "I couldn't help but hear that you've got a number of them."

"I suppose," I muttered sheepishly.

"Like what?"

I was silent for a moment. I really hated reciting a list of my powers — it always felt like bragging. That said, it was clear that Ursula was waiting on me to say something.

"Invisibility," I said. "Flight. Super speed."

I stopped there. It wasn't a list of all my powers by any means, but it felt like enough. (Not to mention the fact that one of my powers — the ability to heal people — wasn't something I fully controlled yet and thus shouldn't be tallied up with the rest of my talents.) Ursula just stood there, quietly looking at me until it became evident that I had nothing more to say on the subject.

"Well, don't be shy," she suddenly urged. "Let's see what you can do."

"Uh, okay," I said, caught flat-footed by her request for a demonstration.

I turned invisible. Ursula, seemingly taken by surprise, swiveled her head back and forth, looking for me.

"Where are you?" she asked.

Rather than respond, I quickly stepped over to where she had gotten the receptacle earlier. Picking it up, I coughed softly to get her attention, then came walking back toward her with the container in my hand.

Ursula's mouth fell open, and then she clapped her hands in glee. From her perspective, it must have looked like the container was just floating in midair.

# INCARNATION

Feeling eyes on me, I glanced in the direction of Rune and Endow; the two Incarnates were staring at me intently.

I marched around Ursula once with the box in my hands, then placed it back where I'd gotten it. As I began walking back to Ursula, I noticed Rune and Endow continuing to watch me. No, not just watch me — *track* me. With a start, I suddenly realized that they could see me, even though I was still invisible.

I filed that information away for future reference as I came abreast of Ursula and made myself visible again.

"Impressive," she noted. "Show me something else."

I nodded, and then rose a few feet into the air. I hovered there for maybe five seconds, then came back down. Ursula, smiling broadly, seemed absolutely delighted. Next, I made a duplicate of myself — another Jim — but only for a few seconds. (The ability to duplicate myself was a completely new power that I wasn't fully comfortable with yet, mostly because of some objectionable side effects, so exhibiting it for Ursula was actually impetuous and impulsive.) Now getting in the swing of things, I was about to shift into super speed when a familiar voice sounded.

"Okay," Rune bellowed. "Jim showing off to impress a pretty girl means it's obviously time for us to go."

"Hey!" I blurted out. "I wasn't showing off."

Ignoring me, Rune turned to Endow and said something I didn't catch; she simply nodded in response. Seemingly satisfied, Rune looked in my direction.

"You ready, hotshot?" he asked.

"Sure," I muttered, noting that Ursula giggled at his comment. She then quickly lifted a hand up to her face, with her thumb and little finger extended toward her ear and lips, respectively, imitating a phone.

"Call me," she mouthed silently and winked.

# INCARNATION

## Chapter 13

We reappeared in our suite, with me laughing at the absurdity of Ursula's last gesture. I seriously doubted that this place even had phones.

Ignoring my giddiness, Rune took a seat in the chair he'd occupied earlier and asked, "So what are your impressions so far?"

"About what?" I shot back, switching my vision back to normal as I sat down on the couch.

"Endow. Mariner. That's two Incarnates you've met. Do you think either of them could be a killer?"

"I've spent practically zero time with them," I admonished. "You guys keep hoisting me off on *laamuffals* while you go off and talk about matters above my pay grade."

"I'm sorry if it seems that way," Rune said sincerely. "We're actually trying to determine the best way to help you figure this thing out."

I sat up. "What do you mean?"

Rune sighed. "Everyone's promised to cooperate, but you have to understand something. These are some pretty powerful individuals, and they're not used to being questioned about their comings and goings. So, despite pledges to the contrary, it's possible that several of them may bristle at being treated like suspects."

"So what, I've got to be an iron hand in a velvet glove now?"

Rune shrugged. "It wouldn't hurt. Plus, you have to remember that we were all coming here for other reasons, which have nothing to do with the murder."

"Can you expound on that?"

# INCARNATION

Rune seemed to consider for a moment how best to answer. "I think I mentioned before that Incarnates are required to come here — to Permovren — regularly, and during those mandatory visits, we check most of our powers at the door, as you put it."

"I remember," I confirmed with a nod.

"Part of the reason for that is to intentionally make us vulnerable, so that we remember that not everyone is like us. Not everyone can do what we do. Not everyone is power incarnate."

"So this is basically an exercise to keep Incarnates humble — to make you mindful of where you come from. Remember your roots."

"Something like that," Rune acknowledged with a chuckle. "But it's also an opportunity to mete out justice."

I gave him a curious look. "How's that?"

"If an Incarnate abuses the trust placed in them, if they use their powers irresponsibly, coming here during times like these presents the rest of us with an opportunity to deal with them."

"Couldn't you do that anyway — without having to come here?"

Rune shook his head. "You don't fully comprehend the might we possess. An Incarnate wielding his full array of powers is impossible to bring down — even by the combined might of all his fellows. Trying to do it outside of a place like Permovren would be cataclysmic on a cosmic scale. Being stripped of the bulk of our *sivrrut* is the only way it can be accomplished, and even then it would probably take at least two of us to get the job done."

"I think I understand," I said. "Inside Permovren, a rogue Incarnate is like a guy with a revolver. Outside, he's more like a man with his finger on the launch button of a nuclear bomb."

"Try a supernova," Rune suggested, "because that's the comparative level of damage we're talking about."

"Wait a minute," I blurted out as a new thought occurred to me. "Why are we jerking around talking about the best way to bring down an Incarnate? We already *have* a way to do that."

Rune nodded, a downcast expression on his face. "The Kroten Yoso Va."

"Exactly," I said, feeling pleased with myself.

The Kroten Yoso Va was an ancient artifact that could be used to siphon power from one object and transfer it to something else. In our previous adventure together, it had been used to subdue Rune and transfer his *sivrrut* to a second-rate magician called Diabolist Mage (and as a result had made the Diabolist capable of extraordinary feats.) Ultimately, we'd been able to prevail against the Diabolist, and Rune had taken possession of the Kroten Yoso Va (which was ideal, since, when I touched the darn thing, it had responded by roasting my hands).

"Unfortunately, we can't use it," Rune remarked with a grimace.

"Why not?" I demanded. "I mean, this is what it's for. It was specifically created to keep Incarnates in check. Those are your exact words. Situations like those are the entire reason why the damn thing exists! Why wouldn't you use it?"

"Well for starters, it's not here," Rune explained. "I left it on Earth."

"Go get it," I said flatly.

"I can't," he said a bit timidly. "We're, uh… We're stuck here."

"What?" I barked.

"We've sealed Permovren off — me and the other Incarnates, that is. No one gets in, no one gets out until we find the murderer."

## Chapter 14

I stared at Rune in shock, and then bellowed, "When were you going to tell me this?!"

"I wasn't trying to keep it a secret," he insisted. "It just didn't come up."

"Why would it?" I demanded. "Why would I asked if I've been kidnapped?"

"Kidnapped?" Rune repeated. "You're laying it on kind of thick, don't you think?"

"What I'm thinking is that I should have asked a lot more questions before agreeing to help you. I'm also trying to figure out which is worse: that no one can leave until the killer is caught, or that you left the only weapon capable of stopping said killer."

Rune shook his head dismissively. "Even if I'd brought the Kroten Yoso Va, we couldn't have used it."

"Sure we could have," I countered. "We could use it to siphon off the power of the other Incarnates, then simply read their minds to figure out who's the murderer."

"That's a might-makes-right argument, Jim. It's equivalent to you holding a bunch of your friends at gunpoint and saying, 'One of us is a murderer, so I'm going to tie all of you up and interrogate you one by one until I find out who the killer is.' Does that sound okay to you?"

I frowned in distaste at the imagery his words had invoked and admitted, "Not really."

"Plus," he went on, "I've heard it said that for supers to lose their powers is like losing a limb."

I nodded. "That's true. For supers, your powers are a central part of who you are. Losing them is akin to being maimed."

"Well, it's a million times worse for Incarnates. So in my scenario, in addition to hogtying and interrogating your friends, you also hack off body parts until you find out what you want to know. And when it's over — even if you get the bad guy — all you can say to the innocent ones is, 'Sorry about that, but I'll sew these arms and legs back on and you'll be good as new.'"

"Okay, I get it," I said, rubbing my temples.

"They'd never trust you again," Rune continued. "Likewise, if I used the Kroten Yoso Va like you suggest, the other Incarnates would never trust *me* again. And I have to deal with these people for eons — maybe even eternity."

"I said I get it," I stressed. "So we can't use the Kroten Yoso Va."

"That's what I've been saying," he announced with a self-satisfied air.

"What are you looking so smug about?" I asked. "You've trapped us inside with a murderer, kept the guy you brought on board to investigate in the dark, and intentionally discarded the only weapon that could stop the killer."

"Geez, Pollyanna," he muttered. "You're just all rainbows and unicorns."

"Funny," I said sarcastically. "What are you going to say if the murderer kills you?"

Rune seem to ponder this for a second, then shrugged and offered, "Avenge me?"

# INCARNATION

## Chapter 15

According to Rune, the next item on the agenda was for me to meet with his fellow Incarnates. However, that was slated for a little later, so we had some time to kill. Leaving Rune in the living room, I headed to my quarters.

Once inside, I dashed around the place at super speed to get a better feel for the layout. (Although I had been in here earlier with Sayo, I hadn't had an opportunity to look around.) Ultimately, I ended up in the bedroom, where I stretched out on the bed.

One of the benefits of being in a place like Permovren was that physical needs were practically nonexistent. Being outside of space and time, you didn't get tired, hungry, thirsty, or the like. That said, even though I didn't have any physical fatigue, mentally, I was exhausted; it felt like the first time I'd been alone in days.

Relishing the quiet and the solitude, I closed my eyes and rubbed my temples, thinking I would just lie there and rest for a few minutes…

\*\*\*\*\*\*\*\*\*\*\*\*\*\*\*\*\*\*\*\*\*\*\*\*\*\*\*\*\*\*\*\*\*\*\*\*\*\*

I woke to a thunderous booming noise, like two wooden bowling pins being rammed together repetitively. After a few seconds, I realized that it was coming from the front of the apartment. More to the point, I recognized it as someone knocking (or rather, banging) on my door.

There was a bathroom connected to my bedroom, and I dashed inside at super speed to make sure I was presentable and then headed to the door. I yanked it open and stood there, dumbfounded; directly in front of me was a giant hand there, at least as tall as me (and which had apparently been doing the knocking). A moment later, the hand vanished, leaving me with an unobstructed view of the main living area, where Rune was sitting on the couch.

"Oh great, you're awake," he said, coming to his feet. "And just in time. The others are waiting for us."

"What others?" I asked.

Rune gestured with his hand, and the room furnishings altered. Gone were the items in the middle of the room, like the couch and easy chair. In their stead was a decent-sized conference room table at which six people were seated, three to a side.

Three of them I knew: Rune, who took a seat on the right side at one end; Endow, who sat across from him; and Mariner, who sat next to Endow. The other three were all men (and presumably Incarnates), but I had never seen any of them before. To my great surprise, however, they all had nametags in front of them.

The one seated next to Mariner appeared to be in his late thirties and sported a short, neatly-trimmed beard. He was dressed in what looked like a full-length black leather duster, under which he wore a formal white shirt with a jabot. On his left forearm he wore an odd mechanical contraption that seemed to have a lot of moving parts — gears, springs, and so on — all of which were completely exposed. On his head sat a black top hat with a clock in its center. Finally, running clockwise around the brim of the hat was a bronze-colored metal gear or cog about two inches in diameter. The nametag in front of him said "Pinion."

Across from Pinion sat a man wearing a long-sleeved blue T-shirt and black pants whose nametag read "Reverb." Based on his frame, it looked like he worked out regularly, but he was an Incarnate, so who knew? On his head was a shock of white hair that normally would have made me think of someone in their senior years, despite the contrast with his physique. However, I found it impossible to even estimate an age based on appearance, because his entire face beneath the eyes was covered by a metallic mask. In fact, the mask didn't just cover his face — it appeared to be bolted onto it, with rivets running along the edge of his jawline.

Finally, between Rune and Reverb was a fairly heavyset man dressed in what I took to be monk's robes. He had short, iron-gray hair and appeared to be in his early forties, and — like his colleagues — seemed to have one distinctive and notable attribute: he was surrounded by something like a soft, blue-white glow. No; upon closer inspection, it was actually more like an electrical charge that pulsed along his exterior. His nametag said "Static."

I took all of this in over the course of a few seconds. There was a chair at the end of the table near Rune and Endow that I presumed was intended for me. Without waiting for an invitation, I came forward and sat down.

I spent a moment looking around the table, not sure what was expected or where to start. Then I mentally shrugged and decided that it probably didn't matter.

"I've already met some of you," I began, "but for those I haven't, my name's Jim. I'm here to help with the incident that occurred."

"You mean Gamma's murder?" asked Pinion, speaking with a crisp British accent. "There's no need to be circumspect. You can say it: *murder*."

"The murder, then," I said, acquiescing. "Did Gamma have any enemies?"

# INCARNATION

Mariner chuckled. "There's an old saying among our kind: Incarnates don't have enemies."

I frowned. "What's that supposed to mean?"

"Enemy implies an adversary," Endow explained. "Someone or something capable of competing with you or doing you harm. Gamma was an Incarnate."

"And because almost nothing can harm an Incarnate, you don't have enemies," I concluded. "There's a fallacy in that logic, but we'll come back to that. For now, though, I'll phrase the question a little differently: who didn't like her?"

"She wielded almost limitless power for eons," said an odd, almost robotic voice. "There would be many who did not like her."

I looked around in bewilderment. I hadn't seen anyone speak. In addition, the voice had seemed to come from all around us.

I reached out to Rune telepathically. <What the hell was that?>

<Reverb,> he responded. <He speaks by taking ambient sound — the rustle of cloth, the squeak of a chair, even breath sounds — and playing around with things like modulation and tonality until he obtains a reverberation approximating the word he wants.>

<Seems like a lot of work,> I surmised. <Why doesn't he just speak?>

<Because the sound of his voice would kill you.>

I kept my face passive, but found myself shocked by Rune's statement. Thankfully, telepathic conversation occurs much faster than verbal communication, so no more than a second or two had passed since Reverb had spoken.

# INCARNATION

"Okay," I said after recovering from my surprise, "this discussion seems to be going nowhere, so I'm just going to be blunt. Gamma's dead, and someone at this table killed her — *sans* yours truly, of course."

"That's something we've already established," Static chimed in. "I thought you were here to provide new information about her death."

I didn't respond to Static immediately. Instead, I found myself intrigued by the fact that I was picking up emotional vibes from him: sadness and melancholy, but also confidence and resolve. It was in stark contrast to the other Incarnates, from whom I didn't detect anything at all on an empathic level.

"He's got to ask questions before he gets new information," Rune said, somewhat coming to my rescue. "You can't expect miracles. After all, he's not an Incarnate."

This got a few laughs from those gathered, and bought me time to come up with my next question.

"When I mentioned enemies a minute ago," I noted, "I think Endow pointed out that it's not necessarily someone who wants to do you harm. It can also be someone competing with you."

"You mean like a rival?" queried Pinion. "Again, Gamma was a *Chomarsus*. She didn't have any."

"But who stood to gain from her death?" I clarified.

"No one," Rune stated, shaking his head. "At least, no one here. We don't inherit the *sivrrut* of our deceased fellows or anything like that."

"So is there anyone who *isn't* here who benefits from her dying?" I asked.

# INCARNATION

Mariner let out an exasperated sigh. "Is that really important? I mean, we've already determined that the killer must be one of us. Why does it matter if someone not at this table derived a benefit?"

"Because typically when there's a murder, there's a motive behind it," I explained. "If you find the motive, you oftentimes find the killer. And it may not be about who gains from her death. Maybe it's just plain old revenge?"

"Revenge?" Reverb repeated (although the voice seemed to come from Rune's chair).

"Yeah, revenge," I reiterated. "Maybe she stole someone's boyfriend. Maybe she filched your grandmother's cookie recipe. Maybe she hired away your pool boy. Maybe she…"

My voice faded as a new thought popped into my brain.

"All of you have *laamuffals*, right?" I asked.

"All but the Inscrutable," Static confirmed, inclining his head toward Rune. "Before you, that is."

I didn't bother correcting him. Instead, I focused on the issue that had sprang into my head.

"So if that's the case, where's Gamma's *laamuffal*?" I asked.

There was silence for a moment as a number of those present exchanged glances.

Finally, Endow spoke, saying, "We're not sure. He vanished around the time of Gamma's death."

I frowned. "Why is this the first time I'm hearing this?"

"Hearing what?" asked Reverb.

"That there's another suspect besides you Incarnates," I growled.

"I don't think anyone ever viewed him as such," Rune said.

I looked around the table incredulously. "Gamma's killed, and at the same time, her servant goes missing," I grumbled. "And none of you felt that was suspicious? Have you never heard the saying, 'the butler did it'?"

Pinion let out a bark of laughter. "Ha! He was a *laamuffal* and she was an Incarnate! Do you investigate fleas for the murder of a human being?"

I pointed a finger at him. "See, that's the problem right there: your arrogance." I then let my gaze go from face to face, declaring, "It's not lack of experience that's resulting in your poor deductive capabilities. It's hubris."

All of a sudden, Pinion pounded a fist on the table — in anger, I initially thought, and then I realized he was laughing.

"Ha!" Pinion belted out. "I like this one, Rune! He's funny. You should have brought him around ages ago."

Assuming that he was probably construing me as a *laamuffal*, I was mildly irked. One day, when this was all over, I'd have to find a way to bring all these Incarnates down a peg or two.

*All these Incarnates?* I thought as a crucial fact unexpectedly dawned on me.

"Hey," I began, getting the table's attention. "Where are the rest of you?"

"The rest?" Static echoed.

I nodded. "Yeah. Rune said there are about a dozen of you, but there are only six around this table, so where are your other compadres?"

# INCARNATION

"They won't be joining us," Rune answered. "They weren't here when the murder occurred, so they aren't suspects."

"And with Permovren sealed off," Reverb added, "there's no way for them to enter now."

"Not that they would *want* to," I noted. "I mean, who would want to be locked in here with a killer, right?"

That particular commentary was greeted with nothing but silence and blank stares.

"Anyway," I said, "I still don't understand why you people are having such a tough time cracking this case. I mean, you can warp reality, bend time and space... Why can't you just go back in time and see who the killer is, send Gamma a warning, or something along those lines?"

"You're forgetting that Permovren exists outside of space and time," Rune chided. "There's no *time* here for us to go back *to*."

"Well, there's *some* form of time here — even if it's only subjective," I insisted. "We're not all frozen in stasis."

"Yes, there is a sequential flow of events here," Endow said, "but it's not time as you understand it."

I gave her a perplexed look, clearly conveying my incomprehension.

"Let me see if I can explain this in a way you can grasp," Pinion interjected. "Imagine you have two temporal distorters."

I frowned. "You mean time machines."

"Sure," he said, waving a hand dismissively. "Now let's say one can slow down time until a second feels like hours or even days. The other can take you back in time — *real* time, not subjective — exactly one minute."

"Okay," I mumbled, nodding.

"So let's assume you've played around with the first temporal distorter and stretched a second out until it subjectively felt like half a day," Pinion said.

"I'm following," I replied.

"But now, you want to use the second temporal... uh, time machine, to go back one minute within that subjective time frame."

I thought about it for a moment. "So in real time only a second has gone by, but subjectively — from my perspective — it's been twelve hours, and now I want to go back one minute within that twelve-hour, subjective time frame."

"Yes, that's the scenario," Pinion said with a nod. "But you won't be able to do it because the second time machine only goes back one minute in *real* time. It can't take you back within your *subjective* time frame, because only one second has passed."

"So you're basically saying that time here in Permovren is like the one second that's subjectively stretched out into a longer time period," I summed up. "And the ability of the Incarnates to go back in time is akin to the second time machine, so that you can't go back in time within this place."

"Exactly," Pinion declared.

"Hmmm," I muttered. "I hate to say it, but that actually makes sense."

# INCARNATION

## Chapter 16

My meeting with the Incarnates broke up shortly after Pinion's explanation about time. They really didn't have much more to impart, although they did agree that I could talk to their respective *laamuffals*.

After they were gone, Rune brought our original furniture back with a wave of his hand and we both sat down.

"So," Rune began, "initial thoughts? Impressions?"

"Honestly, my first thought was that, despite all the time you've spent on Earth, you've never seen a cop show," I groused. "Don't you know that you aren't supposed to question suspects together?"

Rune chuckled. "These are Incarnates. They were going to give the same responses regardless of anything else, and I figured this would save you time."

"Oh, you mean the time that doesn't exist here? *That's* what you were trying to save me?"

He just stared at me for a moment, then muttered, "Ever the wise guy, I see."

"Anyway," I said, "I'm shocked none of you considered Gamma's *laamuffal* as a suspect. What was his name, by the way?"

"Cerek," Rune replied. "And again, only another Incarnate could have done this, so we eliminated him as a suspect."

"Well, *I* wouldn't have eliminated him," I stressed. "I can see a guy flippin' out after millennia of servitude. In fact, I can see all of your *laamuffals* having a bellyful of kowtowing."

"Simmer down, Spartacus," Rune said. "No need for a slave rebellion just yet. Besides, as I said earlier, *laamuffals* aren't these sycophants you're portraying them as."

I raised an eyebrow. "No?"

"No," he insisted. "They're more like...familiars."

"Familiars?" I repeated, skeptically.

"Yeah, like a wizard's owl, or a witch's black cat."

"And you think that's better?" I asked. "Are you listening to yourself?"

"It's certainly better than this master-and-slave interaction you keep describing."

"Fine, it's not master and slave," I growled. "It's more like Dracula and Renfield."

My comment caused Rune to burst into laughter, and a moment later, I joined him. He and I didn't have quite the same banter that I enjoyed with my mentor Mouse, but it was close enough.

"Honestly," I said after the laughter died down, "with everything you Incarnates can do, I don't know why you need servants in the first place."

"Well, sometimes you just need someone to bounce ideas off of," Rune said. "Or, after you've done something, to tell you whether you did as good a job as you thought."

"In other words, what good is it to be all great and powerful if there's nobody to appreciate it."

"That's the sycophant argument again, and I'll stress — as I did before — that you've got the wrong idea. It's not really about having a servant. In fact, sometimes it's just about having someone to talk to."

"Because it gets lonely at the top, right?"

Rune simply gazed at me for a moment, then said, "Are you sure you're not an Incarnate? Because even with my full slate of powers, I couldn't manage to be as cynical as you about everything."

Now it was *my* turn to chuckle at *Rune's* comment. I had to admit that, although we obviously clashed on some things, I liked him.

"Hey," I intoned, "I've got a question for you — a little off-topic."

"Shoot," Rune said.

"A couple of times now I've heard you referred to as 'inscrutable.' Why is that?"

He nodded, seeming to ruminate momentarily before answering.

"You've probably noticed by now that we Incarnates tend to have names that highlight our attributes," he stated. "In my case, even among Incarnates, much of what I do is mysterious or unknown. On top of that, I tend to eschew traditional Incarnate conventions, like having a *laamuffal* — even though I defend the practice. As a result of all that, I'm occasionally referred to as 'The Inscrutable Rune.'"

I thought about this for a moment, then asked, "So does that mean that the duties of the other Incarnates are well-known?"

"Not really," Rune admitted. "For instance, I'm not sure I know anything about Static's obligations — for all I know, he does nothing. However, he wields the power of an Incarnate, so I don't question it."

"So if you don't know what the others are supposed to be doing, how do you know they're doing anything at all?"

Rune seemed to ponder the question for a moment, then said, "There's a certain level of order, shall we say, that Incarnates are required to maintain throughout the cosmos. If one of them is slacking off, we can often detect it by the amount of *dis*order that arises."

"Interesting," I mused.

"Now, getting back on point," he stated, "what's next on your agenda?"

I shrugged. "Not sure. Normally in a place like this, I like to spend some time getting the lay of the land. Being a teleporter, I can only go to places I've seen, so…"

I didn't finish, but Rune picked up where I left off.

"You'd like to see more of the castle so you can fully utilize your powers, if necessary," he said.

"Something like that," I admitted. "Might be worthwhile to combine that with a search for Gamma's *laamuffal*, Cerek."

"Makes sense," Rune conceded.

"Are there any places that are off-limits to me?"

Rune appeared to contemplate the question for a few seconds before responding with, "Yes and no. There are places you are forbidden to enter, but with respect to those, you won't be able to get in. So basically, any room you can get into is fair game."

"Is anyone likely to stop me?"

Rune's brow crinkled. "What do you mean?"

"Well, I'm new here, nobody knows me, I've got no credentials… I'm just trying to figure out if there's like a neighborhood watch that's going to call Permovren PD on me if I just go wandering around."

"I get it," he said. "You want some kind of badge of authority. That's easy enough."

Rune brought his hands together and held them there for a second, almost as if he were praying. Then he opened his hands up in a gesture reminiscent of someone opening a book. There, resting on his palms, was what looked like an oddly-shaped badge of some sort with a red jewel in the center and a length of chain attached.

He handed the badge to me, saying, "Here you go, Officer."

# INCARNATION

## Chapter 17

I left Rune in our suite, where he was allegedly working on something related to the murder. Thus, on my own for just about the first time since entering the castle (and with my "badge" around my neck and tucked down the front of my shirt), I started exploring.

I'd been in situations like this before — basically, unfamiliar surroundings — and my standard operating procedure was to turn invisible so I could move about while being as unobtrusive as possible. (I would typically phase as well, becoming insubstantial, so I could travel freely and unhindered for the most part.) Thus, phased and invisible, I set about trying to get a feel for my new environs.

As I had already realized, the castle was enormous. As I went through it, I noted rooms as big as houses, hallways as wide as thoroughfares. It had been constructed on an enormous scale, as if designed to house thousands of people.

As it was, however, I saw very few individuals. Most that I observed wore the same livery as the majordomo, Dalmion. However, I came across a small number of others, haphazardly, that I assumed to be *laamuffals*, if only because I wasn't aware of who else might be in the castle.

All in all, while I enjoyed the time I spent going through the place, my exploration of the castle wasn't particularly noteworthy, aside from two events.

The first was an encounter with two Incarnates — Reverb and Mariner. I had actually just come through a wall and was floating about five feet above the floor when I found myself in a chamber with the two. They appeared to be engaged in deep conversation, but stopped talking and turned in my direction once I entered the room. It was eerily reminiscent of my prior experience with Endow and Rune; although I was invisible, it was plainly evident that Reverb and Mariner could see me, as they kept their eyes on me the entire time I was in their presence — right up until the moment I reached (and phased through) the wall that was on the opposite side of the room from the one through which I'd entered. (Presumably their conversation resumed once I made my exit.)

The other incident that occurred took place shortly after I left the chamber where Reverb and Mariner were talking. I had just phased through a wall and found myself in a totally dark room. To be truthful, however, it could have been a broom closet or an airport hangar for all I knew, because — even when I cycled my vision through the entire spectrum — I still couldn't see anything and therefore had no idea how big the space was. (To put that in perspective, there is *always* some portion of the light spectrum that will allow me to see what's around me. Ergo, being stuck in total darkness was almost a shock.)

The inability to see anything was unnerving enough, but in addition to that, I got the impression that I wasn't alone. I wasn't picking up on any emotions and when I reached out telepathically, I didn't encounter another mind. However, I couldn't shake the feeling that I was in the presence of...something.

Finding the whole thing somewhat unsettling, I quickly moved forward with the expectation (and hope) that I would soon phase through a wall and find myself outside the weird room. It didn't quite happen that way.

Normally, when I phase through a wall, there is, of course, a transition through some type of building material:

wood, stone, drywall, what have you. I go through *something* to get to the other side. In this instance, I didn't pass through anything; I just suddenly found myself in another part of the castle. (One with adequate lighting, I might add.) I frowned, thinking how bizarre my exit had been. It was less like I'd left the place, and more like the room had just dumped me out.

I didn't have time to dwell on the incident, however, because I'd been in my current location only a few seconds when Rune materialized in front of me.

"Where have you been?" he almost demanded.

"Exploring," I replied.

"Exploring *where*?" he asked. "I couldn't find you."

I shrugged. "I don't know. It's not like these rooms have name plates or placards next to them."

Rune groaned in agitation.

"Come on," I remarked. "I wasn't gone *that* long."

"Oh, really?" Rune chided. "I thought the murderer had gotten his next victim."

I let out a strained laugh, unable to tell if he was serious or not.

"We'll come back to that," he said after a moment. "Right now, we need to go. The others are waiting on us."

I raised an eyebrow. "What, is this going to be another powwow with all the suspects? Because I need to tell you, I think it'll just be a waste of time."

"Not in this instance," Rune said. "We think we may have figured out how Gamma was murdered."

# INCARNATION

## Chapter 18

A short time later, I found myself in a large chamber — maybe fifty-by-fifty feet in size — along with the six Incarnates. Although the place was square-shaped, Rune and his colleagues were in the middle of the room, loosely gathered in a circle that was about fifteen feet in diameter.

I stood in a corner of the room, wondering what the heck was going on. I hadn't had an opportunity to ask Rune any questions; he had simply made a gesture and "Poof!" — we were here. Upon arrival, he had told me to stand back and observe, then rushed to the other Incarnates. Now as I waited for Rune and his contemporaries to do something, I glanced around the room.

I had been wrong when I had initially called the castle drab and unadorned. During my exploration, I had come to realize that each room typically had at least one embellishing feature. Sometimes it would be a mural painted on a wall, or a vaulted ceiling. Other times it would be something as simple as a rug in the middle of the floor.

In this particular instance, I noticed that the walls themselves (which were made of stone) had been meticulously sculpted to depict various battle scenes. On one wall, a group of archers on a hilltop were raining arrows down on charging cavalry. On another, a minotaur wielding an axe was in battle against some kind of tree monster. In yet a third, men armed with halberds were facing off against…well, I honestly didn't know what they were, but they looked like bipedal squids wearing armor and carrying spears.

# INCARNATION

At this juncture, my attention was drawn back to the Incarnates, who had tightened up their circle so that it was now perfectly symmetrical. All six of them were standing completely still (so still, in fact, that I wasn't sure they were breathing), like soldiers at attention with their feet together and hands by their sides. And then — in unison — they all turned their hands so that their palms faced inward, toward the center of the circle.

Almost immediately, I noticed something happening. Light began to form in the center of the circle, initially bright and effervescent but then dimming considerably. As I watched, the light quickly began coalescing and taking on shape — human form, in fact. At a guess, I thought the figure appeared feminine, and I was proven right a few moments later when the light vanished altogether, revealing a woman standing there.

She was about medium height and had a slender frame. Her petite features were accentuated by rather pale skin and dark eyes. Her shoulder-length hair started off achromatic at the front near her forehead, then segued into streaks of color — going from left to right across her head like a rainbow — before becoming colorless again at the back. (And when I say like a rainbow, the streaks in her hair literally mimicked a rainbow: red, orange, yellow, green, blue, indigo, and violet.)

<Rune!> I said, reaching out telepathically for my friend. <What is this? Who's that woman?>

<That's Gamma,> he replied.

<Gamma?> I echoed, as I glanced at the woman. But Gamma was dead. She couldn't be here, unless...

<I thought you guys couldn't manipulate time in here,> I said, feeling certain that was the only way the dead *Chomarsus* could be making an appearance.

# INCARNATION

<That's not what this is,> Rune assured me. <We're just reverse engineering the events leading up to her death, Incarnate-style.>

*Reverse engineering?* I thought.

I turned back to Gamma. As I looked her over, I realized that I'd misspoken when I said that she was "standing there." It didn't appear that her feet were actually touching the floor. Even more telling, I suddenly noted that I could actually see through her, as if she were a ghost.

I had additional questions for Rune, but before I could ask them, Gamma went into motion, drawing my attention. Spreading her feet apart, she appeared to brace herself and then raised her arms until they were parallel to the ground, palm-outward. At the same time, her face became a mask of concentration as, lips pursing, she frowned with effort.

Frankly speaking, she looked like a mime trying to push an invisible wall. I got the impression that she was struggling against something, which I simply wasn't able to see. And then it hit me.

Like other Incarnates, Gamma's name was a reflection of her attributes. Gamma rays, I knew, were at one end of the electromagnetic spectrum, beyond the ability of the human eye to perceive. Fortunately, that wasn't a limitation for me, and I quickly cycled my vision through the spectrum until I found a range that allowed me to see what was happening.

Gamma appeared to be in a pitched battle of some sort, with rays of light firing out from the palms of her hands. Unfortunately, I wasn't able to discern who her opponent was, as the beams she produced vanished when they passed outside the circle formed by the Incarnates present. That said, her adversary, whoever he or she was, seemed to give as good as they got, as noted by the fact that similar shafts of light were being fired back at Gamma. Even worse, they seemed to be taking a toll.

I had to admit to being impressed by what I was seeing. Like a bomb expert rebuilding a detonated device, the Incarnates were somehow visually reconstructing what had happened to Gamma. It was a mind-blowing display of their abilities, once again highlighting just how powerful they truly were.

On a whim, I reached out empathically. As expected, I detected no emotions from Gamma; she wasn't really there, so no surprise at being unable to detect anything. Likewise, I didn't pick up any vibes from Rune and his fellow Incarnates — except Static. The feelings were much the same as before (basically sorrow and resoluteness), but they were almost overshadowed by anger this time. (I did notice, however, that in this part of the spectrum, all of the Incarnates — not just Static — seemed to have a luster about them. In fact, Static seemed to have an additional glow — an inner shine near his chest area — as if he were trying to one-up his colleagues.)

My gaze went back to Gamma, who had seemingly started to wilt under the attack, letting out what appeared to be a groan of pain. Wincing, she stopped her own assault, while the attack on her appeared to intensify. Then, her eyes went wide, as if she'd suddenly had an epiphany, and she screamed, "No! No! No! Cerek!"

Catching motion with my peripheral vision, I looked away from the scene in the middle of the room. Much like Gamma had done a moment earlier, my eyebrows went up in surprise at what I saw.

One of the archers sculpted into the wall had stepped down to the floor of the room.

# INCARNATION

## Chapter 19

It took me a moment to get over my shock, during which time the archer unexpectedly turned toward me, drawing his bow. Immediately recognizing the danger, I automatically went into defense mode and shifted into super speed without consciously thinking about it, just as the statue loosed his arrow.

The world around me went into slow motion. A dust mote floating near me appeared to get stuck in midair. Gamma's facial expression froze in place. Most importantly, the arrow that was fired at me seemed to get mired in place. Nevertheless, being able to estimate its trajectory, I got out of its flight path — and not a moment too soon.

I had barely stepped aside when something whizzed by me, almost grazing my chest. I stood there, momentarily stunned by what had just happened, for two reasons.

First, when I'm at super speed, there's practically *nothing* that whizzes by me. Nothing. Frankly speaking, I'm just moving too fast at that stage for anything like that to happen.

The second reason I was jolted related to the identity of the object that had come close to tagging me: the stone archer's arrow.

Relative to me, it had moved at what I presumed was its "normal" speed.

Somewhat stupefied, my mind raced for a moment, trying to figure things out. Had I lost my powers — somehow shifted out of super speed? But a quick glance around revealed that Gamma (as well as the dust mote I'd noted earlier) still looked frozen. That meant the statue had sped up!

As I was coming to this conclusion, I looked back at the statue and noted that it had nocked another arrow. More importantly, several of its fellows had also stepped down to the floor. In fact, all around the room, the images sculpted into the walls were coming to life. And they all appeared to be moving at super speed.

"Heads up!" I shouted toward the Incarnates. "We got company!"

At the speed I was going, my voice probably sounded like rapid-fire nonsense. Truth be told, however, I probably could have saved my breath, as — moving almost in synchronized fashion — the Incarnates broke away from the circle they had formed. The image of Gamma immediately vanished, and then I had no more time to focus on anything other than fighting for my life.

The archer who had previously shot at me was drawing a bead on me with his second arrow. I phased, becoming insubstantial, just as the arrow came flying toward me. As expected, it passed harmlessly through my chest. A moment later, someone thrust a spear through my neck from behind, while two more arrows passed through my midsection.

I was still phased and thus managed to escape injury, but an unsettling fact quickly came to light: as each weapon/projectile passed through me, I noticed that I was starting to feel the contact, despite being insubstantial. With the first arrow, I hadn't felt anything, but with the spear came the sensation of being lightly touched with a feather. The last two arrows had generated a sensation along the lines of someone lightly tracing a line on my skin with a fingernail.

# INCARNATION

I fought to stay calm as the horrible truth dawned on me: whatever was fueling these sculptures had not only granted them super speed, but was also giving them the power to affect me while phased.

Deciding to go on the offensive, I focused on the first archer I'd seen and teleported his head to a corner of the room. Much to my surprise, the archer's body — instead of collapsing to the ground — calmly nocked another arrow.

Of course — these things weren't actually alive. They were being animated by some force, directed by some other being's will. They didn't really have eyes, brains, and so on. Thus, merely removing its head was not enough to incapacitate it, as it would have done with a living creature.

Taking a different tack, I phased one of the archer's legs; off-balance, it toppled over and smashed to pieces as it hit the floor. Now that it was gone, I noticed two of its fellows nearby also taking aim at me. Understanding that they were quite likely the source of the two arrows that had been aimed at my gut, I telekinetically grabbed them and smashed the two statues together like a wrecking ball slamming into the side of a building. They fractured and crumbled to bits almost immediately.

I watched for a moment, half-fearful that the shattered fragments would somehow reassemble themselves. Thankfully, they stayed where they'd fallen, appearing now to be nothing more than broken chunks of stone.

Feeling a little flush with victory, I was giving myself a mental pat on the back when another spear-thrust lanced me through the shoulder blades and sent the tip of the spear poking out through my chest. This time, the contact felt like someone tapping me on the shoulder to get my attention. This thing was getting real serious, real fast.

Spinning around, I found myself facing one of the armored squid-things; it was holding the weapon that, presumably, I'd just been run through with. Deciding not to waste time, I telekinetically grabbed it by the legs. Wielding it almost like a mace, I swung it around aggressively, slamming the squid creature into two others of its kind before forcefully smashing it to the floor in a maneuver that would shatter it completely.

Finding myself with a small reprieve, I quickly swept the room with a gaze and noted that an intense battle was going on all around me, with the statues rabidly attacking the Incarnates. That said, there was an incredibly eerie quality to the conflict, and it took me a second to figure out what it was: unlike in the movies, where people are always screaming battle cries during skirmishes, none of the combatants were making any noise.

The statues, of course, were…well, statues; it wasn't surprising that they were rather muted. However, the Incarnates also battled in silence, saying nothing as they fought the stone figures. But, despite the lack of war cries, the fight was no less intense.

Mariner wielded a watery sword that, oddly enough, seemed to be bathed in flames. Whenever he touched an attacker with it, the statue would immediately be blasted apart as water violently erupted from a score of places along its frame. (It put me in mind of a balloon being rapidly filled with water until it bursts.)

Pinion didn't have a weapon, but the gear that had previously circled the brim of his hat was now on the floor and had grown to a size I pegged at six feet in diameter. It rolled around the room with the force of a locomotive (and seemingly at Pinion's direction), purposefully crushing and grinding anything in its path (which, thankfully, was limited to the attacking statues).

All of the other Incarnates were engaged in the fight as well, but before I could get a more specific idea of what they were doing, the entire room suddenly shook like an earthquake had struck as a fulminant and agonizingly shrill noise rang throughout the place. It was like nails on a chalkboard — if the nails were replaced with daggers and the chalkboard was your brain — magnified a million times over.

But it wasn't just a physical sound that I heard; I also perceived it in my head — in a way that had nothing to do with my physical senses, making me realize that the sound was reverberating across all possible levels: mental, physical, metaphysical, and more.

Most significant of all, however, was the fact that the noise was, across the board, indescribably painful — even though I was still phased. Physically, it felt as though someone had taken a jagged blade and sliced every inch of my flesh down to the bone. Mentally, it rattled around in my skull, trying to jar my brain loose from its moorings. The resulting headache it caused was both immediate and massive, as well as blinding.

Groaning loudly, I doubled over in pain, blinking almost spasmodically as I tried to clear my vision, while all around me I detected a sharp clattering, like a bunch of rocks being dumped out of a wheelbarrow.

I got the impression of motion somewhere near me, then heard Rune ask, "You all right?"

Nodding, I clamped down on my pain receptors and slowly straightened up as the agony receded. With the physical discomfort gone, my vision returned and I looked around the room, noting with some surprise that the floor was covered with rubble. It was as though someone had taken a jackhammer to the floor and broken it all up. Without being told, I understood that — whatever had happened — it had destroyed the rest of our statuary assailants.

"Why'd you do that?" I heard Mariner ask. Turning in the direction of his voice, I saw him addressing Reverb. "I was having fun."

Looking at Mariner, I couldn't help but think that he had a very different definition of "fun" than I did: there was the handle off a blade sticking out of his right eye.

On his part, Reverb didn't respond. Instead, he pressed a hand firmly against his left jaw and sort of pushed in, reminiscent of a guy massaging a sore spot after taking a punch in the chops. I didn't know if Reverb had a similar definition of fun as Mariner, but I did notice that he had three arrows sticking out of his chest.

Curious as to whether the other Incarnates had suffered injury as well, I was about to do a quick tally when, without warning, the room began to shake. No, it wasn't the *room*; it was the shards on the floor — the remnants of the statues. They were vibrating en masse, and a moment later, they began to emit a soft red glow.

I was still staring at them, trying to figure out what was going on, when I unexpectedly found myself back in the living room of our suite, along with Rune. A moment later, a sound like a gigantic, muffled cough echoed through the castle, accompanied by a rumble that shook the floor and walls.

I looked at Rune and asked, "What just happened?"

## Chapter 20

Rune refused to answer any of my questions until he looked me over and confirmed for himself that I was okay. Thankfully, that didn't take long (although it required me becoming substantial again), at which point I once more asked, "So what just happened?"

"If you're talking about the noise we heard after we arrived back here in the suite, that was an explosion," he explained.

"An explosion?" I muttered in surprise. "What kind of explosion?"

"What kind of explosion? A cute one, with rabbit ears and a big fluffy tail," he deadpanned. "What do you mean, what kind of explosion?"

"I mean, what caused it?"

"I'd have thought that was obvious: the killer."

"So now he's just trying to murder us all?" I asked, using the term "he" to encompass both genders since we didn't know if the killer was male or female.

"With an effort like that?" Rune said derisively. "Unlikely. That was just to destroy clues."

"Huh?" I muttered, frowning. "Okay, maybe you just need to start at the beginning."

"Fair enough," he said with a nod. "I got the initial idea after you mentioned us going back in time to look at Gamma's murder. As was explained before, we couldn't do that, but it occurred to me that we could do something almost as good: reverse engineer the crime scene."

"The Incarnate Bomb Squad," I chimed in. Rune frowned, obviously not comprehending, so I explained the reference.

"That's actually a pretty good analogy," he said when I was done. "I probably would have compared it to arson investigation myself, but they ultimately involve the same thing: analysis of a crime scene in order to determine what happened."

"How'd you find out where Gamma died?" I asked.

"We always knew *where* it happened," he replied. "We sensed it. But since we couldn't go back in time, we didn't know exactly *what* had happened — until you gave us the idea."

"Glad I could be of service," I intoned. "Also, the way you guys reconstructed everything was impressive."

Rune made a dismissive gesture, downplaying my praise. "As I stated before, when it comes to Incarnates, much of what we do can be most likened to magic, which is why many on Earth consider me a magician of sorts. In terms of reverse engineering what happened, you have to understand that, visually, we Incarnates see the world very differently than you do. But much like a bomb expert might investigate a crime scene in order to figure out what caused an explosion, we were able to examine the area of Gamma's demise and ascertain how events unfolded."

"So you did the *Chomarsus* equivalent of looking at shrapnel, structural damage, and debris to understand what happened," I summed up. "And then you recreated it."

"In essence."

"So what's the story with the statues coming to life?"

"That was the killer's handiwork, of course."

"So it was an ambush?"

"Not exactly," Rune said. "They weren't really there to hurt us. They were there to keep us from seeing what happened to Gamma."

# INCARNATION

"How can you be so certain?"

"Because they weren't anywhere near powerful enough to cause real harm."

"Speak for yourself," I chided, then relayed how the statues went into super speed and appeared to affect me to some extent even while I was phased.

"As you're probably starting to realize," he stated, "you've got an impressive power set, but it's not remotely comparable to what an Incarnate can do."

I nodded, not needing to be convinced — especially when, upon reflection, I recalled that the Incarnates had been moving at super speed as well while fighting the statues.

"That reminds me," I said. "Is everyone okay? I couldn't help but notice that a couple of people didn't come through unscathed." I then mentioned Reverb and Mariner.

"They're fine," Rune assured, "as is Static, who got jabbed in the leg with a spear."

"Good to know," I said. "Guess some people are just stoic about getting a knife in the eye."

Rune laughed. "You have to understand — that wasn't even a light skirmish for an Incarnate. For Mariner, that was probably akin to playing with a kitten and accidentally getting scratched."

I pondered on that for a moment, and then asked my next question. "So what happened to them — the statues, I mean. One moment, they were all around; the next, they were in pieces."

"That was Reverb," Rune answered. "He spoke."

I looked at him in surprise. "He destroyed them with his *voice*?"

"Yeah. Frankly speaking, you're lucky to be alive. Fortunately, Reverb had the presence of mind to turn away from you so that his words weren't uttered in your direction. Still, there aren't many outside of Incarnates who can claim to have heard his voice and lived."

"Well, it's not like I got away without a scratch," I reminded him. "Reverb's voice almost rattled my teeth out of my skull. Tell him to use his inside voice next time instead of shouting."

"Ha!" Rune laughed. "That wasn't a shout. That was a whisper — and a barely audible one, at that."

I blinked, taken aback by the implications of Rune's statement. Needless to say, if that was a whisper, I didn't want to be anywhere around if Reverb ever decided to speak in a normal tone.

"So," I said, getting my mind back on track, "was it also Reverb who made the shattered statues start glowing?"

"No, that was the murderer," Rune declared. "I brought us back to our suite just before the remains of our attackers exploded."

"Okay," I droned, mulling that over. "I understand what happened now, but why step up his game and try to kill everyone at the end by blowing us up?"

Rune shook his head and gave me a patronizing look. "Did you forget? The killer is an Incarnate. He was in there with us."

I reflected for a moment on what that meant. "So you're saying he *wasn't* trying to kill everyone in that explosion?"

"Correct. The explosion was intended to destroy the room where Gamma was killed. Using your bomb squad analogy, it's like destroying the crime scene, as well as any evidence like bomb fragments, debris, and shrapnel."

"Wow," I muttered. "You're better at this detective stuff than you let on."

"Not really," he confessed. "This was just one of those times when it was easy to put two and two together."

"Still, that explosion only happened minutes ago."

"Enough time to figure out that we wouldn't be able to recreate the scene of Gamma's death again. Figuring out the rest was kind of elementary after that."

"And extremely helpful," I noted. "Since we know that the murderer basically set up the ambush and booby-trapped the room, maybe we can trim the list of suspects by figuring out who has an alibi with respect to those things."

"I already know the answer to that," Rune declared. "No one."

"Huh?" I mumbled, confused.

"No one has an alibi," he stated.

## Chapter 21

I looked fixedly at Rune for a moment before speaking.

"Bearing in mind what just happened in the room where Gamma died," I said, "are you honestly telling me there's no one we can exclude from our list of suspects?"

He let out a sigh of exasperation. "It's not that easy."

"Sure it is," I countered. "Let's just take it from the top, starting with who knew that you were planning to reverse engineer the crime scene."

"Everybody," Rune stated. "We planned on everyone participating, so they all knew."

"And who knew when it would happen?"

"Again, everybody. You can't have participation if the participants don't know when to show."

"So, between you telling them about it and the actual showtime, who had an opportunity to set something up?"

"This is where it gets complicated," Rune explained. "Look behind you."

Frowning, I turned around — and then stared in surprise. There, leaning against the back wall, was Rune. However, rather than his current garb, this version of my companion was dressed as a stereotypical cowboy. He wore jeans, a leather vest, cowboy boots, and a ten-gallon hat. (And just to complete the picture, he had a wheat straw sticking out of his mouth.) Smiling, he raised a hand and tipped his hat to me.

Somewhat dumbfounded, I spun back around to find the "original" Rune still in place. I opened my mouth to speak, but Rune held up a palm in my direction, cutting me off.

"Wait for it…" he droned.

A second later, Mariner appeared at a spot about ten feet to Rune's right. Quite honestly, I was surprised that he appeared hale and whole — not like a guy who'd had a blade in his eye just a few minutes earlier. (In fact, I had mentally envisioned him sporting an eye patch the next time I saw him. Instead, the only thing different about his present appearance was that his coat was open, revealing sculpted pecs and abs, along with water-formed trousers.)

Mariner gave Rune a steely look. In all honesty, I don't even think he realized I was in the room.

"Really?" Mariner said. "We were even, but you want to start things up again by hurling lightning bolts around my quarters? Use them to etch your name on the ceiling?"

"Sorry," Rune said flatly, not sounding sorry at all. "That was an accident."

"Oh, yeah?" Mariner grumbled. "So's *this*!"

He gestured, and something like a pike — but made of water — flew at Rune, who batted it aside. Unfortunately, he swatted it in my direction.

Acting on instinct, I phased as the water-pike broke into pieces — all of which came hurtling at me. Reflecting on what had happened with the statues in the other room, I experienced a moment of worry, but the remnants of the broken weapon passed through my insubstantial form without me feeling anything. As I turned to watch, they struck the wall where cowboy-Rune had been standing, gouging deep chunks out of it.

I swung back around to where Rune and Mariner were still facing off. The former was still slapping his colleague's projectiles aside, but the resulting fragments were practically destroying the room, tearing through furniture, walls and more.

Without warning, a geyser erupted beneath Rune's feet, carrying him up until it slammed him into the ceiling, then letting him drop unceremoniously to the floor. He was up in a moment, hurling something like a snowball at Mariner, who — now wielding what appeared to be a watery whip — struck it in midair. Almost immediately, the whip froze, with the frost traveling not only the length of the weapon, but up Mariner's arm to the elbow.

Mariner made a jerking motion with his arm, shaking off the frost. Even more, his whip was now encased in flame, much as his sword had been earlier. He drew his arm back, plainly intent on using the whip to inflict a punishing strike on Rune, whose hands were now glowing as he prepared to employ some new weapon (or defense) of his own. However, before either made another move, Endow appeared, standing between them.

"Enough!" she roared, glaring at the two men.

"Okay, okay," Rune said sheepishly, holding up his hands — which were no longer glowing — defensively.

"Yeah," added Mariner, whose whip had also vanished. "We were just goofing off."

"Well, you two — with your horseplay and juvenile pranks — need to stop before you destroy this castle," she scolded.

"Fine," Mariner acquiesced. He waved a hand, and the entire room returned to its former, undamaged state, with the walls once more whole and the furniture intact. He then smiled at Rune and said, "Until next time, Inscrutable." And then he vanished.

Endow turned to Rune expectantly. "Well?"

"I was just demonstrating to Jim how none of us have an alibi," he explained. "Basically, we can practically be in two places at once, and we can affect things outside our presence."

"Like making lightning strike in a colleague's room?" she chimed in, causing Rune to look a little embarrassed. She then looked in my direction. "So, was Rune's little spectacle beneficial?"

Becoming substantial again, I shrugged. "I don't know. It certainly didn't help eliminate any suspects, which is what I was gunning for. In essence, Rune's demonstration shows that no one has an alibi."

"Well, are there other options for narrowing the list of suspects?" Endow asked.

"Nothing immediately comes to mind," I admitted. "Under ordinary circumstances, I might be able to use my empathic abilities to read the room and try to whittle the list down that way. Unfortunately, I can't really sense the emotions of Incarnates. In fact, Static is the only person I've been able to pick up on."

As I finished speaking, I noticed Rune and Endow exchange a glance.

"What?" I asked, realizing something unspoken had passed between the two of them. "What aren't you telling me?"

"Nothing really," Rune said. "It's just that we should have realized you'd sense something from Static."

"Because of his relationship with Gamma," Endow added, "it's no surprise that — emotionally — he's having trouble keeping things contained."

"So, were they an item?" I asked. "Dating? Was he in love with her or something?"

Endow gave me a look that hovered somewhere between aversion and repugnance. I got the impression that she wanted to wash my mouth out with soap. No, it was more like she wanted to wash it out with soap, scour it with a steel brush, and then rinse it with bleach.

After a few moments of uncomfortable silence, Endow said, "She was his mother."

My eyes widened in surprise. "Oh."

Well, that explained Endow's look of distaste and disdain.

"Wait a minute," I blurted out as a thought occurred to me. "They were mother and son? Don't you Incarnates have some kind of 'No Nepotism' policy?"

The other two exchanged another glance, and then Rune put in, "Uh, yeah…we're circulating a draft around the office."

Ignoring him, Endow stated, "It's uncommon, but not unknown or unprecedented for two Incarnates to be related."

"So which of them was an Incarnate first?" I asked.

"Gamma," Rune said. "She was an Incarnate long before Static was even born."

"Is that important?" Endow inquired.

"Probably not," I admitted. "How's he taking her death?"

"Just as you've seen," Rune said. "No real outward display, but apparently some internal turmoil, which you'd expect — even from a *Chomarsus*."

"Hmmm," I muttered. "Why 'apparently'?"

"Huh?" Rune said.

"You said that Static 'apparently' has some inner turmoil," I explained. "Wouldn't you know for sure?"

# INCARNATION

"No," Rune declared. "I based my comment on your assessment."

"Incarnates typically don't try to read each other that way," Endow chimed in. "Just as we don't try to read each other's minds."

"Is it considered rude, or something?" I asked.

"It's not so much that," Rune answered, shaking his head. "It's just that it's another exercise in futility. Like reading their minds, you'll only pick up what a *Chomarsus* is willing to share, and even then you won't know if it's a sincere emotion."

"Unless it's a situation like this," I opined, "where someone like Static is dealing with something incredibly emotional."

"Yes," Endow agreed. "I recall it happening with Gamma before, when one of her other children died."

I frowned, thinking. "She had other children?"

"Yes," Endow replied. "Long before Static, however."

"Natural causes," Rune said. "They grew old and died."

My forehead wrinkled as I reflected on that. Parents outliving their kids had to be painful — even for beings like Incarnates.

"Okay," I conceded. "I can see how Gamma would have found that distressing." I didn't even want to think about what it must have been like for Static to help recreate her last moments.

"You have to understand," Endow remarked. "As Incarnates, we'll still be alive after the sun goes out. We all had to make our peace with the fact that we would outlive loved ones."

"Not if the murderer has anything to say about it," Rune interjected.

"That brings up an interesting point," I said. "We haven't established motive, so we don't know why Gamma was killed. Without that, there's no guarantee that the murderer will strike again."

Endow looked at me with a curious expression. "Are you suggesting that we just do nothing?"

"Not at all," I assured her. "It's just that I've been operating under the assumption that the killer will be looking for his next victim, and that may not be the case. Gamma may have been the only person he wanted out of the way."

"So you're saying that, after blowing up the room where Gamma was killed, we may never hear from him again," Rune summed up.

"It's possible," I acknowledged, and then frowned. "Speaking of that room, why can't you guys recreate it?"

"What do you mean?" Endow asked.

"Well, the murderer destroyed that place because he didn't want us seeing what ultimately happened," I said. "But just like Mariner repaired everything in here" — I made a gesture encompassing our current environs — "why can't you guys put the room back the way it was so we can finish seeing what occurred?"

"It's a bit more complicated than it appears at first blush," Rune stated. "What Mariner did here was basically just a repair job. You can liken it to a handyman coming to your house to fix a hole someone knocked in the wall. Say he puts a drywall patch over the hole, slaps some joint compound on it, sands it down and then paints it. When he's done, the wall looks the same as it did before, but it's not exactly the same because now there's a covered-up hole in it, for one thing. Likewise, we can repair the room so that it looks the same as before, but it won't be the exact same room."

"And because it's not the same room, you can't reconstruct the crime scene again," I concluded.

"Precisely," Endow confirmed. "Maybe if we had our full *sivrrut*, but not with our current limitations."

"Okay, but you guys still have all kinds of abilities," I countered. "Can't one of you read some tea leaves or look into a crystal ball and see what happens in the future — see if there's another murder?"

"Again, we're outside of space and time," Rune reminded me. "There's no 'future' here, as you understand it, for us to see."

I sighed in exasperation. "You know, for a group of near-omnipotent beings, you guys have made helping you impossibly hard."

"Of course," Rune chirped. "Do you know how boring life is when everything is easy?"

# INCARNATION

## Chapter 22

Since revisiting Gamma's last moments was now out of the question, I really only had one clue to follow up on: her last words.

"She was shouting 'No' and 'Cerek,'" I said to Rune and Endow. "I didn't see anyone else during the reconstruction, but it implies that her *laamuffal* was in the vicinity."

"It sounds plausible," Endow conceded. "Do you think he was involved in the attack on her?"

"I think you guys likened it to fleas murdering a human," I replied. "Seems unlikely."

"I don't think Endow was suggesting that Cerek killed Gamma," Rune clarified. "I believe she was implying that he might have assisted the murderer."

I let that roll around in my head for a second. "Seems more probable than him doing the deed himself. Was he unhappy working for Gamma?"

"Like all *laamuffals*, he was dedicated to her," Endow said.

"Spoken like a typical boss," I declared, then uttered in a mocking tone, "'My employees all love me.'"

"But in this case it was true," Rune insisted.

"How do you know?" I asked. "Did he give her a 'World's Greatest Boss' mug or something? Because they only give those out to people who deserve them."

Rune crossed his arms in agitation. "Okay, wise guy, here's the skinny on *laamuffals*: they have incredibly long lifespans, during which they look how they want to look. They dress how they want to dress. They eat what they want to eat. They get to see the wonders of the universe. And if they don't like it, they can quit at any time.

On our part, if they don't have the loyalty and commitment an Incarnate requires — and we'll know, because we can sense it — we'll simply release them from service with no hard feelings."

"Wow," I muttered, impressed. "For a guy who doesn't have a *laamuffal* of his own, you knocked it out of the park on the job description."

"Thanks," Rune said, looking smug.

"Although you left out the part about working side-by-side with an omnipotent killer," I added. "Guess any applicants will need to read the small print."

Rune shook his head in disgust. "Anyway, what's your next step?"

"Trying to find out what I can about Cerek," I replied. "Despite what you said, maybe he wasn't getting along with Gamma."

"But who would know that besides him and Gamma?" asked Endow.

"His colleagues," I answered.

Endow looked pensive for a moment. "You mean the other *laamuffals*?"

"Of course," I remarked with a nod. "Employees always commiserate and complain about the boss."

# INCARNATION

## Chapter 23

Endow and Rune asked for a little time to arrange for me to see the *laamuffals*. That was fine with me; I felt the need to unwind anyway. Telling them to come get me when they were ready, I teleported to my bedroom.

I popped up next to the bed and essentially collapsed onto it. As before, I felt fine physically, but mentally it seemed like the walls were closing in. This situation had a lot of moving parts, and in an effort to get my arms around things, I decided to take a quick tally of what I was working with.

Seven suspects (if you counted Cerek).
Six nigh-omnipotent beings.
Five *laamuffals*.
One killer.
No alibis.
No body.
No motive.

I groaned aloud. This was way more than I signed up for when I agreed to help Rune, more than I felt capable of dealing with. The one silver lining was that it kept me so preoccupied that I didn't have time to think about my girlfriend, Electra. (Or rather, *ex*-girlfriend, since she broke up with me.) But now that she had come to mind…

\*\*\*\*\*\*\*\*\*\*\*\*\*\*\*\*\*\*\*\*\*\*\*\*\*\*\*\*\*\*\*\*\*\*\*\*\*

I spent a little time simply lying there and daydreaming about fun times I'd had with Electra: hanging out with our friends, going on dates, and so on. We hadn't been broken up for very long — less than a day, in fact, at the point in time when I'd come to Permovren with Rune — but it felt much longer.

I was still reflecting on my relationship with Electra (and pondering if she was regretting dumping me) when an unusual sound reached my ears. It was something like twigs being snapped and put me in mind of wood crackling in a campfire.

At the thought of a blaze, I immediately jumped up from the bed. The sound seemed to be coming from the sitting room of my apartment, so I shifted into super speed and dashed there immediately.

Much to my relief, nothing was on fire. Or, more specifically, none of the *furniture* was on fire. As I looked around, however, I did detect the source of the crackling: one of the walls was burning.

Fire, of course, is almost universally recognized as a hazard. Thus, I was about to shout for help when I noticed two things. First, the fire on the wall wasn't spreading; it seemed confined to a relatively small area. The second thing that caught my attention was that the conflagration on the wall wasn't just a single blaze. From what I could see, it consisted of numerous flames that seemed to be arranged in a pattern.

All of a sudden, the flames began to die down in a unified fashion, and I stared in surprise at what was revealed as they began disappearing.

Without taking my eyes off the wall, I reached out telepathically for Rune and located him in the main part of our suite.

<Rune!> I bellowed telepathically. <You better get in here!>

Rather than acknowledge the message, he simply appeared in my apartment, materializing next to me.

# INCARNATION

"What is it?" he asked anxiously.

Rather than answer, I pointed at the wall where the fire had been. The flames were gone now, but had left behind scorched and smoldering marks that were easily identifiable.

They were words, and they formed a chilling message:

STAY OUT OF MY WAY

# INCARNATION

## Chapter 24

Rune was able to repair the wall with a wave of his hand. Afterward, we reconvened in the living room of our suite. (Endow had apparently left shortly after I went to my room.)

The scorched statement had clearly been a warning, and we didn't have to guess who it was from. Moreover, in addition to the words actually etched on it, the wall also conveyed another message: the killer wasn't done.

"So why now?" I asked. "Why try to warn me off now instead of earlier? He could have done it before that first meeting with the Incarnates, before I went off exploring, before the reconstruction of Gamma's murder. Why now?"

Rune pondered for a moment. "Maybe you did something to tick him off."

"Or maybe it's not something I *did*," I countered. "Maybe it's something I'm going to *do*."

Rune raised an eyebrow. "Such as?"

"What was next on my to-do list?" I asked.

"Talking to the *laamuffals*."

"And is it safe to assume you had to clear that with their bosses?"

"Yeah," Rune stated with a nod.

"So after it becomes known that I want to speak to *laamuffals*, I get a flaming message on my walls."

Rune frowned. "So you're implying that there's something about the *laamuffals* that the killer doesn't want you to know."

"I'm saying that I need to speak to the help as soon as possible."

# INCARNATION

## Chapter 25

Pinion's *laamuffal* was the first one who I spoke with. Much to my surprise, he wasn't human; he was a steam-powered robot who stood about six-foot-six in height and went by the name Gearbox.

We met in a small conference room that Rune had designated for interview purposes. Gearbox — who preferred to stand while I sat — gave straightforward responses to my questions.

"Was Pinion involved in Gamma's murder?" I asked, dismissing with any pleasantries.

"Not to the extent that I am aware," Gearbox responded.

"Would you tell me if he were?"

"I am programmed to be loyal to Pinion."

"So does that mean you wouldn't?"

"It means that I would abide by his wishes. If he were involved in the murder and wished it known, I would speak to that effect. If he were involved and wished it kept secret, I would not divulge the information."

"What if he were involved but did not make his wishes known in that regard?"

"I would seek his opinion."

I pondered for a moment. "How much free will are you granted?"

"I am not restricted in what I may do by either word or deed. However, if you are asking if I may commit murder, I am imbued with a strict moral code that includes an abhorrence of violence toward living creatures. However, I may act in any manner necessary to protect innocent life."

"So you can kill if you so desire?"

"Desire indicates a want or yearning on my part," Gearbox replied. "I do not have such in regard to violence. But to answer your question — yes, I can kill."

"Were you involved in Gamma's murder?"

"I was not."

"Do you know anyone who was?"

"I do not have definitive information in that regard."

"Do you have suspicions?"

"Yes — anyone who stood to gain from her death."

The rest of my conversation with Gearbox went in much the same manner. The upshot of our conversation was that he had built-in loyalty to Pinion, and he did not know who was involved in Gamma's death. As to Cerek, Gearbox didn't know what had become of him, but described him as utterly devoted to Gamma and incapable of anything that would cause her harm.

I received similar responses when I spoke to Konstantin — Reverb's *laamuffal*. A few inches taller than me and built like a weightlifter, he dressed in what I would call a Cossack style, including a kaftan worn over a pair of trousers and a tall, fur *papakha* on his head. Needless to say, he insisted that Reverb had nothing to do with Gamma's death.

"Reverb believes in the sanctity of life," Konstantin assured me.

"So you're saying that he's not capable of killing anyone," I surmised.

"Such an act is beyond him. He would rather die than take an innocent life."

"Didn't feel that way when he spoke while I was in the room," I countered.

# INCARNATION

"Reverb knows precisely how to vocalize in order to take or preserve life," Konstantin insisted. "If you think he was careless in that regard, then I would say it begs the question of whether you are 'innocent.'"

Ignoring his jibe, I asked, "Don't you find it ironic that a guy who can kill with a word holds life in such high regard?"

"It is precisely because he can so casually take life that he reveres it so."

In short, Reverb's innocence was beyond doubt as far as Konstantin was concerned. Furthermore, like Gearbox, he had no clue as to who would want to murder Gamma, who was involved, or what had happened to Cerek. Finally, he was just as adamant as his robotic colleague in the belief that Cerek would never cause injury to the *Chomarsus* he served. That said, I did detect a slight bit of nervousness when we discussed the missing *laamuffal*.

I next spoke with Sayo, but had few questions for her since we had previously spoken. However, there was one thing I had been curious about.

"When we first met," I said, "you correctly identified my quarters and Rune's. How did you know the difference?"

"They're marked," she replied. "As an Incarnate, the Inscrutable's private chambers are distinctly identified. However, I don't think the designation is conspicuous to those whose vision hasn't been augmented."

"Hmmm," I droned. "Are you saying that *laamuffals* can perceive things outside the normal range of vision?"

"Of course. It's a gift, but also makes it easier for us to render service."

"What other gifts are provided to *laamuffals*?"

# INCARNATION

"It depends on the Incarnate, as well as the respective duties of the servant. Certain tasks may require excessive strength, or a keen ear, or a sharp eye."

"Do you know what gifts Cerek would have had?"

"Unfortunately, no," she replied, but — as when we had spoken in my quarters — I started picking up on nervousness and anxiety.

"Do you have any idea what happened to him?"

"No," she said tersely.

Additional questions about Cerek produced responses along the same lines, with Sayo — despite broadcasting uneasiness emotionally — essentially toeing the party line by expressing the belief that Cerek would never have harmed Gamma.

Next was Albion, who served Static. He was about my height, but slimmer, with dark shoulder-length hair that was tied in a ponytail. I put his age at around forty, but it was difficult to tell because — in addition to a gray five o'clock shadow — he had wrinkles and bags around his eyes that gave me the impression that he hadn't slept in weeks. As expected, he had nothing but nice things to say about his boss, but I couldn't help but notice that, in addition to being emotionally jumpy (like Sayo and Konstantin), he seemed to be visibly nervous and unable to hide it.

"Static is, uh, w-w-wonderful," he stammered. "Wonderful, truly."

"Can you see him committing murder?" I asked.

Albion shook his head emphatically. "N-n-no. Never. Absolutely not."

I frowned. Despite their anxiety, I had detected sincerity in the responses given by Sayo and Konstantin.

Albion, however, was so keyed up that it was difficult to discern how truthful he was being.

The same was true with respect to his comments about Cerek, a topic which made him particularly skittish. Like the others, however, he couldn't envision Gamma's *laamuffal* harming her in any way. Ultimately, feeling that there wasn't much new to be gained from him, I brought our conversation to an end. That left me with one last servant to speak with: Ursula.

"Alone at last," she coyly remarked as she came into the room and took a seat.

I chuckled. "I thought you'd be more inclined to say that I'd saved the best for last."

"Po-*tay*-to, po-*tah*-to," she said with a shrug. "So how goes the investigation?"

"Difficult," I admitted. "I haven't been able to eliminate any suspects."

"My fellow *laamuffals* weren't able to assist with that?"

"They all insisted that their respective Incarnates couldn't have done it, and that Cerek wouldn't do anything to hurt Gamma."

She raised an eyebrow. "You don't believe them?"

"They seemed sincere," I stated, "but also apprehensive."

"Can you blame them? Even innocent people get nervous when they have to talk to the cops."

I frowned. "But I'm not a cop."

"Sure you are," Ursula insisted. "You're here investigating a murder, identifying suspects, questioning witnesses. That's Cop Procedure 101. The only thing missing is a trench coat and a partner to trade witty banter with."

"That last would be Rune," I said, smiling. "Although the witty banter is a work in progress."

"Plus he's still a suspect," she reminded me. "Although, now that I think about it, there's at least two suspects you should be able to scratch off your list."

I leaned forward, intrigued. "Who?"

"Static, for starters."

"Why?" I asked. "Because Gamma was his mother?"

"You don't think that carries any weight?"

I shrugged. "Not every parent-child relationship is great. Until very recently, I thought I hated *my* father."

Ursula looked at me in shock, but it was a true statement. My father, Alpha Prime, had been a no-show for most of my life. Because of that — and other reasons — I'd wanted nothing to do with him, but our relationship had undergone a vast improvement recently.

"Before you go there," I continued, "I had no plans to kill him, but you wouldn't have found me wailing at his funeral if something had happened to him."

"And now?"

I sighed. "I accidentally called him 'Dad' a few days ago." This caused Ursula to immediately start giggling. "Anyway, who's the other person you think deserves a get-out-of-jail-free card?"

"Endow, of course," she declared matter-of-factly.

I didn't even bother hiding my skepticism. "Why am I not surprised to hear you say that?"

"Well, have you asked her?"

"Not directly."

"Well, you should, because she'll tell you the truth."

"Of course she will. Murderers always fess up when asked politely, because they don't know how to lie."

113

"It's more like 'can't' rather than 'doesn't know how,'" Ursula stated.

I gave her an odd look. "What are you talking about?"

"Endow," Ursula answered. "She can't lie."

"What do you mean 'can't'?"

"Just what I said. She can only tell the truth."

I made it clear that her comment seemed dubious, stating, "I find that a little hard to believe."

"Ask Rune if you don't believe me," she said. "He'll tell you."

I didn't immediately respond. Instead, I ruminated on the fact that, empathically, her comments were trustworthy and ingenuous — which brought to mind something else I'd noticed.

"So tell me," I began. "Why aren't *you* nervous?"

She looked at me in confusion. "What do you mean?"

"Other than Gearbox, the other *laamuffals* — especially Albion — seemed edgy when I mention Cerek. But when I brought him up a few moments ago, you weren't fazed."

She nodded in understanding, but seemed to contemplate for a second before responding. "Typically, we *laamuffals* bask in the protection of our respective Incarnates. Physical harm is not something we usually have to worry about. But with Gamma murdered and Cerek missing…"

She left the rest unfinished, but I knew what she'd been implying.

"They're worried about getting killed," I concluded. "But not you."

# INCARNATION

"I suppose I trust Endow to be able to handle those things," she remarked with a shrug. "And either she can or she can't. As to Albion, if he's more jittery than the rest of us, that's probably a function of serving Static."

My interest piqued, I asked, "What do you mean?"

"Presumably he's a harsh taskmaster. I just know that his churn rate for *laamuffals* is on the high side. He gets a new one every few years, so it's not unusual for them to be twitchy. Needless to say, Cerek's disappearance isn't helping to settle anyone's nerves."

I drummed my fingers for a moment. "Do you think it's possible Cerek could have done it?"

She frowned. "Killed Gamma? No way — he was completely dedicated to serving her."

"I'm not asking if he *would* have done it," I clarified. "I'm asking if he *could* have."

Ursula snorted in derision. "Uh, nope. He didn't have enough power. No *laamuffal* does."

"But if he *wanted* to harm her," I said, "could he somehow *get* the power to do it?"

She shook her head. "Not really, although you could always poke around the Relic Room and see if something there would suffice."

I looked at her with open curiosity. "What's the Relic Room?"

Eyes twinkling, Ursula stood up and reached across the table, taking my hand and pulling me to my feet.

## Chapter 26

"The Relic Room," Ursula announced proudly, apparently pleased by the fact that I — looking around almost in wonder — seemed to be impressed.

We were in a spacious chamber — the place Ursula had dragged me to after taking my hand. From what I could tell, it consisted of several interconnected rooms, the most dominant feature of which were recessed art niches that covered every wall from floor to ceiling. Each was cylindrical in shape with a domed top, and roughly two feet tall and one foot wide. Moreover, almost every niche was occupied by a curio of some sort — usually a crystal or jewel, but sometimes an unusual stone, metalwork, or some combination thereof.

In a similar fashion, the floors in each room were occupied by what I'd describe as open display cases. Like the art niches, these also contained an assortment of *bibelots*. In addition, most — but not all — of the items in the room seemed to glow softly, bathing the chamber in eye-catching, multi-colored light that was almost breathtaking.

"You asked about *laamuffals* somehow getting additional power," Ursula continued. "The relics in here could be used for something like that."

"So wait," I muttered, dwelling on what she'd just said. "All these items bestow some kind of power?"

"'Bestow' is probably inaccurate. Rather, the relic contains power that someone could use."

"Where do they come from?" I asked, glancing around.

"Many were fashioned by Incarnates. Others, we just don't know."

# INCARNATION

I scratched my temple, thinking. "Why would an Incarnate create a relic? If they wanted someone to have certain powers, why not just give it to them — the way Endow did with that driver?"

"We're not built like Incarnates," Ursula explained. "Physically, we're nowhere near as durable. Having too much of their power conferred on you would burn you to a cinder."

"I get it," I said with a nod. "It's kind of like wiring with too much current running through it."

"Exactly. So the way around that is to imbue an object with the necessary power that the individual in question can access."

"That makes sense," I acknowledged. "So, what's here that might allow a *laamuffal* to power up to the next level and take on an Incarnate?"

Ursula glanced around with a doubtful expression. "I don't know what every relic is fully capable of, but I'm not aware of any that can do what you're suggesting."

"There's got to be something," I insisted. "For instance, I've heard of an object that a person can use to siphon *sivrrut* from an Incarnate and use as their own."

Ursula just stared at me for a moment, and then mumbled, "The Kroten Yoso Va."

"Yes," I said with a nod.

She bit her lip, looking pensive for a moment, then seemed to come to a decision. "Follow me."

Without a word, she turned and began walking through a nearby corridor.

# INCARNATION

## Chapter 27

We ended up in a small anteroom that was about ten-by-ten feet in size. It was connected to the main chamber of the Relic Room via a few narrow passageways, and was — to my surprise — the only place in the area that didn't have the ubiquitous art niches on the walls. (By contrast, even the corridors that we passed through en route had contained the floor-to-ceiling relic niches). In fact, the room was almost completely empty, which — in comparison to the rest of the chamber — gave the place a resolute and reverent atmosphere.

The only items in the room were three ornate metal rods jutting up from the stone floor near what I'd call the front of the room. They were about four feet tall and arranged in a row from left to right. The tops of the of the rods were actually splayed, flaring out into numerous prongs that — upon inspection — appeared to be designed to hold some object in place. As a matter of fact, the center rod actually was holding an item. Recognizing it, I could do nothing but stare at it as if in a daze.

"This is the Optimum Alcove," she stated, making a gesture that encompassed the room. "It's where the Triumvirate is housed" — she pointed with her chin toward the metal rods — "the three most powerful artifacts in existence."

She walked toward the rods, with me, still in something of a trance, following behind her.

"Only one of them is here now," she continued, coming to a halt right in front of the metal poles. "It's—"

"The Beobona Onufrot," I interjected, finally coming back to myself.

# INCARNATION

Ursula gave me a look that bordered more on shock than surprise — as if I were a mongrel dog that had suddenly started discussing particle physics.

"Yes," she finally said with a nod. "That's one of its names. You've heard of it?"

"I've come across it in the past," I stated, staring at the object in question.

The Beobona Onufrot (or "Beobona" for short) was a cylindrical crystal about a foot long and roughly two inches in diameter. I had already known it to be an ancient and powerful artifact — truth be told, it had saved my life on several occasions — but I had no idea that it was connected in some way to Incarnates. (And if what Ursula had just said was true, it was far more powerful than I had ever imagined.) What it was doing in this place, here and now, was completely beyond me; to the best of my knowledge, it still resided in what could best be described as a weird suit of armor back on Earth.

Before I even knew I was going to do it, I reached out and grabbed the Beobona.

"No! No! No!" Ursula screeched as I lifted the crystal from its setting among the prongs. "You can't—"

She stopped mid-sentence as brilliant light of every hue seemed to flare up all around us. Ursula squinted, bringing a hand up to shield her eyes while I, almost as a reflex, cycled my vision to the spectrum until I could see almost normally.

At that point, I realized that the light wasn't exactly coming from around us, but from the corridor we'd used to get to the Optimum Alcove. All of the relics in the niches there — in the entire Relic Room, I sensed — were now beaming as if they contained thousand-watt bulbs. Understanding immediately that this was related to my handling of the Beobona, I hastily put the jewel back. As expected, the light died down immediately, and I cycled back to my normal vision.

"Sorry," I mumbled as Ursula lowered her hand and rapidly blinked a few times.

When it appeared that her vision was normal again, I found her giving me a curious stare.

"Who are you?" she finally asked.

"I'm Jim," I answered, laughing, "as you already know."

"No," she muttered, shaking her head. "I mean, how'd you do that?"

I shrugged. "I don't even know what I did."

"Well, you touched the Beobona, for one thing."

My eyebrows went up. "Is that against the rules?"

"Honestly, I don't know," Ursula admitted. "The thing" — she motioned toward the Beobona — "is here so randomly that it's never been an issue."

"What does that mean?"

"It means the Beobona kind of comes and goes as it pleases," she stated. "It's almost as if the thing's alive."

I didn't say anything immediately, but Ursula's statement actually coincided with my own experiences with the Beobona. The jewel regularly seemed to act as though it had a mind of its own.

"Okay," I finally droned, "but I don't see how that actually translates into look-but-don't-touch."

Ursula let out a sigh of frustration. "I guess you missed the part where I said it was one of the three most powerful artifacts in existence. That being the case, no one has to tell you not to touch it. It's implied."

"Great," I muttered sarcastically. "Scold the new guy for not reading the unwritten rules."

# INCARNATION

Ursula simply looked at me for a moment, then started giggling.

"Okay, fine — you get a pass this time, rookie," she quipped. "Now, back to what I was saying: the Kroten Yoso Va, like the Beobona, is part of the Triumvirate. It can be used, like you said, to take an Incarnate's *sivrrut* and use it for your own purposes. The problem is that it's a lot like putting a three-year-old into a crane swinging a wrecking ball. They have a lot of power at their fingertips, but do they really know what they're doing? They're just as likely to crush themselves as anything else."

"I get it," I said. "Having power is one thing, but knowing how to use it is something else."

"That's why — if used for its true purpose — the Kroten Yoso Va would only be utilized to *take* power from an Incarnate."

I frowned. "You lost me. How's that different than what we were just saying?"

"We were talking about taking an Incarnate's power and *using* it. Although the Kroten Yoso Va lets you do that, if employed as intended, you'd really only *take* power — presumably from a rogue Incarnate who's abusing his authority. That's what it was created for."

"So that raises another question: who created it?"

She shrugged. "No one knows, not even the Incarnates. No one knows how any of the Triumvirate Relics came into being."

"But they're usually kept here?" I asked, gesturing toward the metal rods.

Ursula's head kind of seesawed from side to side for a moment as she said, "Yes and no."

I raised an eyebrow. "Care to explain that?"

# INCARNATION

"Well, as I mentioned, the Beobona kind of comes and goes as it pleases. The Kroten Yoso Va is supposed to go on the right, but it's only here during those times when it doesn't have a Keeper."

"Wait," I uttered a little forcefully. "What do you mean by 'Keeper'?"

"The Kroten Yoso Va is intended to keep Incarnates in check. That being the case, it's not supposed to be in their possession. Ergo, although it *can* be given to a *Chomarsus* for safekeeping, it's usually entrusted to the care of a virtuous and principled individual who'll only use it as intended, and when necessary."

"You mean a normal person."

"Correct."

"But if that's the case, what's to keep an Incarnate from just taking the Kroten Yoso Va from the Keeper?"

"There are allegedly protections in place — presumably something that will drain the power of an Incarnate who tries to take it from a Keeper by force."

"Well, could an Incarnate fashion a knock-off of the Kroten Yoso Va — something that would let him steal *sivrrut* from another *Chomarsus* just like the real thing?"

Ursula seemed to consider this, then shook her head. "I don't think so. To make it that powerful, an Incarnate creating it would have to imbue it with so much of their own potency that they'd drain themselves."

"But what if they had another source of power, to either fuel their knock-off or replenish their own *sivrrut*?"

She frowned in concentration. "Like what?"

"The Beobona," I said, gesturing toward the artifact.

Her eyebrows went up. "It can do that?"

# INCARNATION

Suddenly I wanted to kick myself. I felt like I could trust Ursula, but in my current situation knowledge was power, and I'd basically just given up a key piece of intel.

"Uh, I don't know," I mumbled. "I just remembered you saying it was a powerful relic."

"Hmmm," she muttered, sounding skeptical. "Well, I'm not sure I can answer that. However, there's a legend that says if a person brings together all three parts of the Triumvirate, they'll become, like, a super-Incarnate."

"Really?" I said, trying not to sound as surprised as I felt.

"Yeah, but it's unlikely to happen because, according to rumor, these things move through time," she stated.

I didn't say anything, but that somewhat jibed with my past experience involving the Beobona. At the very least, it had — at one juncture — seemed to be in two different places at the same time. (In truth, based on the known facts, that was probably the case at present.)

"On top of that," she added, "the Third is missing." As she spoke, she motioned toward the metal rod to the left of the Beobona.

"What exactly *is* the Third?"

"That's the thing," she said, sounding exasperated. "No one knows. It's *always* been missing, so nobody has a clue what it is, where it is, *when* it is, or what it looks like."

I mused on that for a moment, then stated, "Maybe that's the point."

"What is?" Ursula asked.

"Maybe whoever created the Triumvirate didn't want them brought together."

"Then why create them at all? Why go through the trouble of creating something like the Third — whatever it is — just to hide it in the dark recesses of space and time?"

I shrugged. "I'm guessing that's something that may only be figured out by the person who brings them together."

# INCARNATION

## Chapter 28

Ursula really didn't have any more information to impart, so she bid me adieu and went back to her duties. I, on the other hand, wanting a little time to digest everything I'd learned, eschewed teleporting to my room and decided to walk back.

I had hoped that talking to the *laamuffals* would clear things up, but it hadn't been nearly as helpful as I'd thought it would be. More to the point, I didn't seem to have learned whatever it was the killer was afraid of me finding out. (Unless it was something too subtle for me to pick up on.) That said, I'd found the information Ursula gave me on the relics to be interesting, to say the least.

I was reflecting on all this when I caught movement with my peripheral vision. I was passing through a midsized room at the time, which was decorated with a fresco painted on each of the walls. Turning in the direction of the motion I'd noticed, I found myself staring at a wall that depicted a forest scene: towering trees, thick grass, a babbling brook...

Once again, motion drew my attention, and I was caught off guard by the appearance of a man running through the forest. More specifically, he was running straight toward me.

Oddly enough, it didn't immediately strike me as bizarre that I was seeing a figure moving in a two-dimensional painting. Aside from being an obvious sign that I was getting far too accustomed to strange occurrences, my only concern was whether or not he was armed. Thankfully, he appeared to be weaponless, but — bearing in mind the recent episode with the statues — I phased and backed up slightly as he stepped from the wall.

# INCARNATION

He was about my height and perhaps in his late thirties, with hair that appeared somewhat unkempt and a beard that looked a bit scraggly. Likewise, his clothes (which seemed to consist of a pair of khakis and a loose-fitting, long-sleeved shirt) were a bit scruffy as well. Finally, I noted that he was a bit like a ghost in that I could actually see through him.

Almost immediately upon exiting the painting, he began talking to me — imploring, to be honest — and gesturing wildly. On my part, I gave him all due attention, but couldn't hear anything he was saying. In fact, the only sound I could detect was a curious rumbling that seemed to come from all around us. That said, it was pretty clear that whatever he was trying to convey was important.

Giving up on the verbal path, I reached out for him telepathically and found nothing. It was as if, mentally, he wasn't there. Emotionally, however, I was able to home in on him, and was surprised by the wide range (and intensity) of emotions coursing through him: hope, fear, doubt, resolve, anger, loss… The feelings were so varied and ranged such a gamut that one would have almost thought the man had multiple personalities.

"I'm sorry," I finally said, shaking my head. "I can't hear you." For emphasis, I pointed to my ear.

Apparently, the man understood, because he stopped speaking and appeared to reflect for a moment.

"Let me get help," I suggested. "One of the Incarnates can—"

At the mention of Incarnates, the man vigorously shook his head, not just indicating that I shouldn't get them involved, but practically begging me not to. At the same time, I sensed dread and apprehension ballooning in him with frightening intensity.

# INCARNATION

"Okay, okay!" I assured him. "No Incarnates."

The man seemed to relax somewhat, but then began to glance around wildly, as though noticing some change in the environment. It took me a moment to pick up on it, but then I realized what was different: the weird rumbling noise had seemingly come to a halt.

Almost in a panic, the man turned and practically leaped back into the painting. A moment later, he was gone, having disappeared into the illustrated undergrowth.

# INCARNATION

## Chapter 29

I stayed put for perhaps ten minutes, hoping that the man would return and keenly scrutinizing the wall for a clue as to where he'd gone. I received satisfaction in neither regard.

On something of a whim, I extended an arm toward the fresco. To my shock and amazement, it met no resistance when it reached the wall and instead seemed to "enter" the painting and become part of it. Caught completely unprepared by this development, I went so far as to lean forward and put my head into the fresco as well, and found myself actually *in* the forest it depicted. Completely unsettled by what I was experiencing, I hastily withdrew, and was happy to find myself in the "real" world again.

At that juncture, feeling frustrated and eager to speak to Rune (not to mentioned just a little freaked out), I teleported back to our suite.

*************************************

I popped up in the living room — and in the middle of a conversation. Sitting across from each other on the couch and easy chair, respectively, were Static and Rune.

"—hy you roused me?" Static was saying grumpily. "To harass me over minutia that doesn't even matter?"

They both turned in my direction.

"Uh…sorry," I began. "I'll just—"

"Don't go anywhere," Rune said to me, obviously anticipating that I was going to excuse myself. Turning back to Static, he remarked, "It absolutely matters. You're a *Chomarsus*, so there's no need to take shortcuts or do shabby work."

"Fine," Static shot back testily. "It's a waste, but I'll fix it."

A moment later, he vanished.

"What was that all about?" I asked.

"Static being Static," Rune replied.

Not knowing what he meant, I simply stayed silent, and after a moment, he went on.

"You probably don't see it," he continued, "but despite everything that's going on, we Incarnates still have duties. Responsibilities. Even while we're stuck here dealing with a murder."

"I take it someone's not holding up their end?"

"Static," Rune answered, "as if you couldn't tell from what just happened." I merely shrugged, at which point he continued, saying, "You remember Dalmion, who met us when we arrived?"

"The majordomo?" I said. "Sure."

"Well, you probably couldn't tell, but the uniform he was wearing — that all the servants here wear — is also a type of armor. Basically, they also have the job of serving as a fighting force if we're ever attacked."

I raised an eyebrow at this. "This place is at risk of attack?"

"I know, I know," he droned. "Being outside of space and time, it doesn't seem likely. But from my point of view, it doesn't hurt to expect the unexpected."

"Makes sense," I conceded. "So what does this have to do with Static?"

"He was responsible for providing the current batch of uniforms. However, he's inherently lazy, and therefore has a bad habit of taking shortcuts. In this instance, the uniform wasn't armored. So when the servants were going through a recent training exercise, one of them was injured because his uniform — which was supposed to protect against weapons fire — didn't do its job. Static's excuse is that it takes a little longer and requires him to expend more *sivrrut* to make the armored uniform, and since we never come under attack here, he didn't see the need."

"But he's going to fix it?"

"So he says, but this is typical of him. He's like a chef who's baking a cake and runs out of sugar. Instead of going out to get more, he'd rather just use salt because they're both white and look alike."

"Okay," I mused. "I guess that does sound a bit indolent."

"That's just the tip of the iceberg with *him*," Rune stated. He let out a pent-up breath and then, apparently ready to move on, said, "Anyway, how'd it go with the *laamuffals*?"

"Less than stellar," I replied, then gave him a quick overview of the interviews (although I glossed over the part about visiting the Relic Room).

"One thing Ursula said did get my attention, though," I said.

"Oh?" muttered Rune, keenly interested.

"She said that Endow doesn't lie. *Can't* lie, in fact."

Rune nodded. "That's true."

I gave him an incredulous stare. "Is there a reason you wouldn't tell me that?"

"Because she needs to be vetted and eliminated as a suspect through the same process as everyone else — whatever that ends up being."

"But if she can't lie, I can just ask her if she did it and either eliminate her as a suspect or point the finger at her as the killer."

Rune shook his head in a condescending manner. "Just because she can't lie doesn't mean she can't equivocate."

"Huh?" I muttered in bewilderment.

"She doesn't have to give straight answers," he explained. "For instance, many places have laws that allow murderers to be executed, right?"

"Sure," I agreed, trying to figure out where this was going.

"Is that considered murder?"

"No," I responded. "It's legally sanctioned."

"So imagine you ask Endow if she committed murder, but she believes she merely executed a killer."

I chewed on his hypothetical only for a moment before deciding, "She'll say she didn't murder anyone."

"Right," Rune stated with a nod. "Now suppose you try to throw her a curveball and ask her if she's taken anyone's life. But let's assume Endow believes everyone has an immortal soul."

"She'll probably answer that with a 'No' as well," I said. "Basically, she'll find a way to sidestep the question while giving truthful answers."

"Now you're getting it," Rune noted. "She'll equivocate. Of course, that's if she answers at all."

"What?" I intoned. "I thought she had to tell the truth."

"She does," he confirmed. "But just because you ask a question doesn't mean she's compelled to answer. In that respect, she still has a choice."

I contemplated on this for a second. "So you're saying that if I ask Endow something like, say, whether she loves me, she could respond — presumably in the affirmative or negative — or she could just sit quietly."

"First of all, yes — your analogy is spot-on," he declared. "Second of all, don't go there."

"Go where?" I asked, plainly confused.

"Falling for Endow."

His tone was so serious and somber that I started chuckling heartily. Just thinking about the age difference between me and Endow was hilarious, so it was obvious that Rune was making a joke. Thus, it took a few seconds for me to realize that Rune wasn't laughing.

# INCARNATION

## Chapter 30

Following our discussion about Endow, the next pressing issue on my mind was the man from the fresco. I had planned to ask Rune about him, but remembered the fellow adamantly stressing that Incarnates shouldn't be made aware of him. More importantly, I had sensed that the man was trustworthy.

Bearing all that in mind, I decided to forego discussing the issue with Rune and opted instead to confer with another local: Ursula.

\*\*\*\*\*\*\*\*\*\*\*\*\*\*\*\*\*\*\*\*\*\*\*\*\*\*\*\*\*\*\*\*\*\*\*\*\*\*\*

Running her down turned out to be fairly easy. I simply told Rune that I needed to speak to Ursula, and he, in turn, simply glanced away for a few seconds before informing me that she was in her quarters. Then he made what appeared to be a twirling motion with his finger. A moment later, I was in what I took to be a great room, with a sizeable fireplace, lush carpeting, and posh furniture.

Sitting on a nearby love seat, Ursula gave me a smile.

"Oh my — a gentleman caller," she said coquettishly, patting the seat next to her. "You know, guys usually wait a little longer before finding a pretext to see me again."

"Huh?" I muttered, confused.

"We practically just finished in the Relic Room, and you're already asking your friends to ask my friends to ask me if you can stop by."

Laughing, I took a seat next to her. "So Rune reached out to Endow when I mentioned wanting to talk to you. And she, in turn, contacted you."

"Yes, but feel free to cut out the middlemen next time," she teased. "And no need to come up with some flimsy excuse — just say you missed me."

"Unfortunately, it wasn't a pretense," I said, chuckling. "I have a legitimate reason for wanting to see you."

"I don't think infatuation counts," she stated with a kittenish expression.

"Come on," I implored with a grin. "I need your help."

"You're no fun," she pouted. "But okay, what's the problem?"

"I need to show you something — telepathically."

She merely nodded in response, and I reached out and relayed to her my experience with the guy from the fresco.

# INCARNATION

## Chapter 31

It didn't take long to share what had happened with Ursula.

After breaking the telepathic connection, I said, "Basically, I'm trying to figure out who the Fresco Kid is and what he wants."

"Well, he's more of a man than a kid," Ursula noted, "but that's Cerek."

I looked at her in surprise. "It is?"

She nodded. "Yeah. Looks like he's been roughing it for a few days, but that's him."

"So," I droned, trying to put that fact in context, "was that his ghost or something?"

"No, you goof," she teased. "The presence of his ghost would mean that he's dead. That was an astral projection, which means he's very much alive."

"Alive *where*?" I asked. "The Incarnates say they can't find him here, and as I understand it, nothing can enter or leave."

"That's all true," Ursula confirmed.

"So where could he be, then?"

She shrugged. "I don't know."

"Think about it," I urged. "If you wanted to hide from an Incarnate in our present environment, where would you go?"

She threw up her hands in frustration. "There's nowhere you *could* go. A *Chomarsus* can see all the places in Permovren that are accessible, and the *verboten* places are…well, *verboten*."

I thought about that for a moment, reflecting on something I'd recently heard.

"Rune mentioned to me that some places in Permovren are off-limits," I said. "Are those what you're referring to?"

"Yes."

"How many places are we talking about?"

Ursula made a vague gesture. "I don't know. I've never done a full tally."

"How many would you guess?"

"I'm not sure," she muttered, shaking her head. "Let's see…there's the Paragon Potens. The Conflagration Chamber. The Room of Ebon Enlightenment…"

"Hold on," I interjected, as something she said seemed to resonate with me. "That last…"

"The Room of Ebon Enlightenment?"

"Yeah — what is that?" I asked.

"Honestly, you're probably asking the wrong person since I've never been in it," Ursula admitted. "That said, it's supposed to be a place that will, among other things, give you answers to the questions you don't know."

I gave her a look of incomprehension. "What does that even mean?"

"Your guess is as good as mine," she declared. "It sounds like maybe it addresses questions you aren't consciously aware of."

"Like when you found something I subconsciously wanted to see," I suggested.

"I suppose," she softly concurred. "Basically — as the name implies — the room is supposed to bring light to darkness, but I assume that's just a metaphor."

"I'm not so sure," I said, reflecting back on what had occurred while I was exploring. "Anyway, it must be comforting to know that Cerek is still alive, even if we don't know exactly where he is."

"It's a bit of a relief," she admitted.

"I can imagine," I said. "I would find it completely nerve-racking if a friend just disappeared and I didn't know what happened to them."

Ursula stared at me for a moment. "So you're saying that if it were your friend, you'd want to know what happened."

I nodded. "Yes."

"Even if it was something bad?"

"Of course," I replied. "I think that's just human nature."

"I think I've been around Incarnates so long I've forgotten what human nature is like," she said flatly.

"I'm sorry," I intoned, "but I'm not sure what you're talking about."

She merely stared at me for a moment, and emotionally I could feel her wrestling with hesitancy and doubt, as if she was trying to come to a decision about something.

Finally she stood up and said, "Come with me. I need to show you something."

# INCARNATION

## Chapter 32

We ended up back in the Cosmos Corridor, where Ursula once again brought up the dimensional vortex. As before, the same two man-shaped figures were in the beam of light, and I could sense them empathically.

Ursula gestured toward the pair in the light beam. "You said these were your friends."

I groaned noncommittally, not wanting to get into the details of how I knew the two men.

"Unfortunately," she continued, "they don't make it."

She looked at me expectantly, but I simply frowned, not sure what she was talking about.

"They don't make *what*?" I finally asked.

"They don't make it," she repeated. "They don't survive."

"Huh?" I blurted out. "What do you mean, they don't make it? Of course, they make it!"

"Look," she said, pointing to an area farther ahead of the men along the beam of light. I gazed at the region she indicated, noting that the beam seemed to be twisted and distorted there.

"That's some kind of dimensional rift," she explained. "It came out of nowhere, but when these two go through it, they'll die."

Stunned, I simply shook my head.

"No," I insisted. "It's not possible."

"I'm sorry, but it is."

"No, you don't understand," I practically growled. "They make it through. It's already happened."

"Maybe it did," Ursula said, giving me a forlorn look. "However, in this place, nothing is set — not even events in the past. Forces arise, come into play — and things come undone."

I found myself breathing heavily, getting angry.

"Get Endow," I practically demanded. "Tell her to fix this."

"She can't," Ursula stated sorrowfully.

"Sure she can. She can do the same thing she did with that driver — endow them with an ability that will let them survive."

Ursula shook her head. "She won't."

"Well, we won't know until we ask her."

Giving me a sad look, she said, "I already did."

I simply stood there in stunned disbelief, unable to speak.

"I asked her as soon as I realized what was going to happen," she continued.

"And?" I barked.

"She said she's not meant to save those two, and they have to be left to their fate."

*************************************

Fuming and frustrated beyond words, I allowed Ursula to drag me from the Cosmos Corridor and into a passageway outside.

"So what good are they?" I finally said. "What good are these Incarnates and all their vaunted powers if they can't save a couple of guys like that?"

I gestured angrily toward the room we'd just left as I finished speaking.

"You have to understand," Ursula countered. "It may seem like they can do whatever they want, but every Incarnate has duties — obligations they can't shirk. Thus, they can't always do what they want — or what we'd like them to do."

Unfazed by Ursula's rhetoric, I was about to continue my rant when the entire passageway suddenly shook convulsively. At the same time, a familiar sound — physically agonizing and mentally excruciating — echoed throughout the place.

*Reverb!* I thought instantly.

# INCARNATION

## Chapter 33

I found myself gritting my teeth and groaning as Reverb's voice sounded all around us. Ursula, feeling no need to hold back, let out a sonorous, undulating scream of torment while at the same time bringing her hands up to cover her ears.

I immediately shut down my pain receptors. As the noise receded and the place stopped shaking, Ursula swiftly took her hands from her ears and brought them together in front of her, about six inches apart. Her palms, I noticed, had blood on them. It was then that I realized her ears were bleeding.

She seemed to concentrate for a moment, and seconds later an object appeared, floating, between her hands. It was a small triangular prism, maybe three inches long and made of stone. Its surface was covered with strange markings and designs that glowed softly.

No sooner had the prism appeared, however, than we were assaulted by another tortuous cacophony of sound that rattled the walls and floor. Ursula made a harsh gasping sound, then her eyes rolled up in her head. At the same time, the stone prism ceased floating and dropped.

I shifted into super speed, catching the prism before it struck the floor. (Somehow I doubted that it would break, but didn't feel the need to take chances.) Wanting to keep my hands free, I slipped it into a pocket and then — after getting into position to catch Ursula — switched back to normal speed. Based on how I'd situated myself, she practically fell into my arms.

I lifted her up, pulling her close to my chest, and quickly looked her over. In addition to her ears, she now had blood running from her nose. Based on that alone, I guessed she was in pretty bad shape. (For all I knew, my own condition was probably just as bad — I simply wasn't feeling it.)

I spent a moment trying to determine my next course of action. I could teleport us easily enough, but — although his voice had resonated all around us — I didn't know exactly where Reverb was. (Truth be told, I didn't even know if he was inside the castle.) If I made a mistake and brought us closer to him, it was likely to be game over for Ursula.

No, rather than make a random guess on teleporting, we'd be better served by finding a place to hunker down. I looked around, eager to find some form of shelter, something that would shield us from Reverb's voice. I didn't see anything nearby except the walls of the passageway.

*Walls!* I suddenly thought.

Once, in the recent past, I had managed to temporarily escape the effects of a villain's weapon by taking refuge *within* a wall. With nothing to lose, it was certainly worth seeing if lightning would strike twice. Mentally crossing my fingers, I dashed to the nearest wall, phased the two of us, and stepped inside.

# INCARNATION

## Chapter 34

Reverb's voice sounded three or four more times while we were in our makeshift foxhole, rattling the walls on each occasion. In total, his verbal assault (for lack of a better term) probably lasted no more than a minute or so, but felt much longer. Needless to say, I stayed put — still holding Ursula — until well after the last time his vocals sent tremors through the place. In fact, we didn't stick our noses out, so to speak, until a familiar voice gave the all-clear.

"You can come out now," I heard Rune say in a somber tone, his voice completely unexpected. "It's over."

Feeling relief, I did as suggested and left the relative safety of the wall, with Ursula still unconscious in my arms. (It didn't occur to me until later that it could have been a trap — someone pretending to be Rune in order to lure me out — but fortunately, such was not the case.) I then made the two of us substantial again, and brought my pain reception back to normal.

In addition to Rune, Endow was also present. Upon seeing Ursula, she rushed toward me, maternal concern etched on her face. Considering what had happened the first two times she'd heard Reverb, I half-expected Ursula to be bleeding from her eyes. Thankfully, she looked no worse than she had when I had stepped into the wall with her, but that didn't necessarily mean anything. (I had tried using my healing power on her when we were in the wall, but — unsurprisingly — I couldn't get it to work.)

I was about to explain to Endow what happened, but didn't get a chance because the next second she and Ursula were both gone.

# INCARNATION

"What the...?" I muttered, startled by their sudden disappearance. Was this how people felt when I unexpectedly teleported out of a room?

"She'll be fine," Rune said, interrupting my thoughts. "Endow will take care of her. But right now we need to go."

"Go where?" I asked.

"Reverb's dead," he stated matter-of-factly. "I need to show you where he died."

"No, wait," I uttered anxiously. In response to the expectant look I then received from Rune, I gestured at my clothes — in particular the areas where Ursula's blood stained them. "I need to change."

Rune's eyes appeared to glow for a second, following which he announced, "You're good."

Glancing down, I saw that the bloodstains were indeed gone. In fact, my clothes looked as though they'd just been dry-cleaned. Nevertheless, I couldn't simply overlook the fact that I'd just had someone's blood on me. Basically, despite the spiffy appearance of my attire, I just didn't *feel* clean.

"It's not enough," I declared. "I need a shower."

"Later," Rune said, in a tone that would brook no naysaying. Then he snapped his fingers and we vanished.

# INCARNATION

## Chapter 35

We popped up in what could have been the field where we'd first appeared in Permovren — if one could overlook the massive crater that hadn't been there when we'd initially arrived. It was a concave depression, about fifty feet in diameter and maybe five feet deep at its lowest point. In essence, it looked as though someone had taken a giant spoon and scooped out a good portion of the ground.

Pinion, Mariner, and Static were already present when Rune and I showed up, standing in a group near the edge of the crater. After we joined them, I stood there for a moment, waiting for them to fill me in.

After a few moments, I finally said, "If anyone wants to tell me what happened, I'm all ears."

"The killer struck again," Pinion replied.

"So I gathered," I stated with a nod. "I was hoping for a little more detail."

"It started in the castle," Mariner noted, "then moved out here almost immediately."

"We assume that was Reverb's doing," Rune added.

"What — moving the field of play?" I asked. "Is there some advantage to being out here?"

"Only if you're not an Incarnate," Pinion chimed in.

I frowned, unsure of how to interpret what I'd just heard.

"There was a good chance that Reverb's voice would have killed anyone in the castle," Pinion explained. "Not wanting to harm any innocents, he seemingly brought the conflict here, where he could fight with less restraint."

"Not that it did him any good," Mariner chimed in as he glanced up at the sky.

Following is gaze, I glanced up but only saw normal sky — a sure sign that Rune's glamour (or whatever he'd done) — was still in place as far as I was concerned.

"His effigy's gone?" I guessed.

"Correct," Rune said.

"And once again, I suppose we don't have a body," I surmised. Rune confirmed this almost immediately with a nod.

"Did any of you sense anything this time?" I inquired.

"Of course," said Static. "As with Gamma, we knew where in the castle Reverb was when the conflict occurred, as well as when he shifted it here."

"Well, if you sensed it, why didn't any of you come to his aid?" I asked.

There was silence for a moment, then Rune intoned, "It's not as simple as that. Contrary to how it appears, we're not all just sitting around waiting for you to solve this for us. We've got other duties to attend to, ongoing obligations to fulfill. We aren't always in a position to just drop everything."

"In essence, the killer arranged for this attack to occur at a time when the rest of us would be preoccupied," said a voice behind me.

I turned to find Endow standing to my rear. It was unclear when she had shown up, but it had obviously been long enough for her to pick up on the conversation.

"That said," Endow continued, "it only took a minute or so for us to get here, but by that time…"

# INCARNATION

She didn't have to finish for me to understand: by the time everyone arrived, it was all over.

"I'm going to guess that there's no way to recreate what happened here," I said, "the way you did with Gamma?"

"No," Mariner confirmed. "The killer took away that option when he left this giant crater."

"What about inside?" I asked hopefully. "The place where this particular incident first started?"

"Same story," Mariner remarked. "The murderer blasted it, the way he did the area where Gamma died."

"Not to be callous," Static suddenly interjected, "but can we forget about what the *murderer* did and focus on what *we* need to do now?"

"No," Rune stated flatly. "I know what you're asking, and the answer's no."

"Come on, Rune!" Static argued. "Two of us have been murdered. We need the Kroten Yoso Va."

"That's you taking a shortcut again," Rune shot back. "We're not there yet."

"Really?" Static muttered skeptically. "With two Incarnates dead?"

"*All* of us will be dead if the wrong person gets the Kroten Yoso Va," Rune argued. "So, bearing in mind that one of us is the murderer, which of us would you propose as the person to take possession of it?"

Static didn't have a ready answer for that. Instead, he looked away in impotent anger, broadcasting a frustrated vibe that you probably didn't have to be empathic to pick up on.

"Look," Rune said after the silence had stretched out for a few moments. "If and when it becomes necessary, we'll use the Kroten Yoso Va. But for now, I wouldn't worry about it."

His statement obviously didn't sit very well with Static, who was about to comment but didn't get a chance.

"How about a compromise?" Pinion hastily suggested. "Rune, you could tell one of us — anyone you like, at your discretion — where the Kroten Yoso Va is. That way, if something happens to you, we'll still have the ability to utilize it, if necessary."

"Sure," Rune acquiesced. "I'll tell all of you, right now." He then looked around at the other Incarnates conspiratorially and said, "It's in good hands. That's where it is."

# INCARNATION

## Chapter 36

Rune's statement about the Kroten Yoso Va essentially brought our investigation of Reverb's murder site to a close. He then transported the two of us back to our suite, at which point I made a beeline for my apartment. Once there, I went straight to the bathroom (tossing my clothes onto the bed along the way) and then took a long, lingering shower.

By the time I finished, I felt clean again. After turning off the shower, I phased; with my body now insubstantial, water fell from me to the shower floor, leaving me dry. I then hurried to the bed and got dressed.

One of the articles I had removed before showering was the badge Rune had given me. I regarded it for a moment after putting my clothes on.

Thus far, no one had questioned my comings and goings (although I was usually in the company of someone else when traipsing through the castle). That made the badge a bit of a superfluous item. In addition, I wasn't accustomed to wearing necklaces or anything along those lines. In short, I was tempted to simply leave it off.

However, Rune had given it to me to alleviate concerns that I had. That being the case, it seemed slightly disrespectful to simply discard it. (Moreover, I barely noticed the thing when I was wearing it, so it's not like it was a burden in some way.) Mind made up, I somewhat reluctantly put the badge back on and again tucked it down my shirt.

No sooner had I done that than I heard an odd rumbling noise. It seemed vaguely familiar, and a moment later, I realized where I had heard it before: the room with the frescoed walls.

# INCARNATION

*Cerek!* I thought.

The sound seemed to be coming from my bathroom. Eager to speak with the *laamuffal,* I hurried back in.

In addition to the shower, the bathroom also contained a double vanity and a sizable mirror, which was still steamed up from my shower. That said, I thought I saw motion in the fogged-up glass that did not match anything I was doing. A moment later, Cerek came out of the mirror like Alice going through the looking glass.

As before, he immediately and anxiously began trying to communicate with me. Similar to our previous encounter, I couldn't hear him or reach him telepathically. His emotions, however, were much along the same lines as before, revealing trepidation and longing, among other things.

"Cerek!" I blurted out. Hearing his name apparently got his attention, because he suddenly stopped trying to speak. "Where are you? What happened to Gamma?"

He gestured wildly, and once again tried to communicate with me by speaking.

"I still can't hear you," I declared, making him once again pause in his antics.

Looking around apprehensively, he suddenly stared at the steamed-up mirror as if seeing it for the first time. Almost in conjunction with this, the rumbling sound (which had continued almost unabated up until this point) seemed to somehow alter, shifting in volume and tone. At that juncture, my eyebrows shot up in surprise, as — amazingly and unexpectedly — I recognized what the sound was.

# INCARNATION

Cerek, who had listened in dread as the rumbling noise changed, abruptly seemed to be on the edge of panic. Still, raising both hands — with fingers outstretched and pointing toward the mirror — he appeared to focus as a look of steely concentration settled on his features.

As I watched, words began to form in the steamed-up mirror. They appeared as one might expect — written one letter at a time in left-to-right fashion, as if by an invisible finger. It was slightly reminiscent of what you might see in a horror movie, and the overall effect was both fascinating and ominous at the same time.

Moments later, in complete alarm and utter frenzy, Cerek hastily bolted back into the mirror. Within a few seconds of his disappearance, the rumbling came to a halt, and once again I found myself almost dumbfounded by what I now understood to be the source of the sound. However, I didn't have time to dwell on it as I focused on what Cerek had written in the mirror.

It was basically two words, one atop the other, with a horizontal line drawn between them:

MOUSES and KLEOP.

# INCARNATION

## Chapter 37

Given that he had seemed to be under time constraints, it was rather apparent that the two words Cerek had left were clues. Frowning, I wandered out of the bathroom and then sat on the edge of the bed, trying to figure out what they meant.

"Kleop" I essentially gave up on immediately. I wasn't sure I'd ever seen it before, couldn't recall ever hearing it spoken, and certainly didn't know what it meant.

"Mouses," on the other hand, was familiar — to a certain extent. It appeared to be an incorrect pluralized form of the word "mouse." I spent a moment debating on whether it was a reference to my mentor, Mouse, before deciding that it had to be a coincidence.

Ruminating further on the issue, I had trouble simply identifying occasions when I'd actually heard the word spoken. I recalled having a computer science teacher who always used "mouses" when referring to more than one computer mouse, but that was about it. Considering that I hadn't seen anything close to a computer in Permovren, I didn't think that application of the term was practical. Cerek had to be referring to something else.

*Was he illiterate?* I wondered. That would certainly explain why he'd used "mouses" instead of "mice." Or was the misspelling intentional, and a clue in and of itself? Likewise, did the line drawn between the two words mean anything?

Groaning in exasperation, I lay back on the bed. There were simply too many questions and not enough answers. Even worse, I didn't even know where to look to *get* answers.

# INCARNATION

I closed my eyes, hoping that a quick catnap would give my brain a much-needed rest and allow me to focus. Still thinking about Cerek (and his need for a grammar lesson on irregular plurals), I slowly drifted off...

\*\*\*\*\*\*\*\*\*\*\*\*\*\*\*\*\*\*\*\*\*\*\*\*\*\*\*\*\*\*\*\*\*\*\*\*\*\*\*\*

I awoke to the feeling that something was off. No, not just off — *wrong*. I sat up at once and looked around, and almost immediately identified what was out of joint: one of the walls of my bedroom was missing.

Three of the walls were fine, but where the fourth should have been there was a thick, roiling mass of darkness. I was tempted to call it a cloud, but it was more solid than vaporous, more akin to tar than smoke.

All of a sudden, the darkness parted and a figure stepped through. "Stepped," however, is an inaccurate description; it was more like the darkness slid under the person's feet and carried them forward, like a moving walkway. That said, it only took me a few seconds to note that the person coming toward me was a man — at least in a broad sense.

He was emaciated beyond belief — so thin that he could almost be a model for stick figures; the tunic and trousers he wore hung loosely off his frame and looked as though they weighed more than he did. His facial features were positively skeletal, dominated by dark, hollow eyes and sunken cheeks that highlighted the bones underneath. (To call him cadaverous would have been generous.) His hair was dark and stringy, and appeared to be falling out in clumps, leaving him with random bald spots all over his head. Finally, his skin was blotchy — distinctly discolored in broad, random patches — as well as afflicted by rashes, warts, and a host of other medical conditions.

As he approached, I felt the hairs on my neck rise. It wasn't merely because of the way he looked; he broadcast a deadly and menacing vibe that had nothing to do with appearance. In short, if he wasn't the killer, he was definitely first runner-up.

My immediate reaction was to telepathically contact Rune — tell him to get his butt in here — but I found myself stymied in that regard. Simply put, I couldn't reach him. I still had my telepathy, but for some reason it now had a very limited range and could extend no farther than a few feet.

*Of course*, I thought. This guy — the killer — was an Incarnate. He was somehow blocking my telepathy.

My next instinct was to teleport — to simply get away from him. To my shock and dismay, despite a valiant effort, I didn't go anywhere. As with my telepathy, the killer was somehow stopping me from teleporting (or maybe just redirecting things so that my end destination was where I started).

I shifted into super speed (thankfully, that ability still worked) and then scrambled to the side of the bed away from him — thereby putting it between us — while phasing at the same time. Recalling what had happened with the statues coming to life, it was a sure bet that neither becoming insubstantial nor dashing around at the speed of sound would be effective against this guy in the long run, but it was better than nothing.

He stopped a few feet from the edge of the bed, staring at me critically with feverish, bloodshot eyes.

"You know who I am?" he asked in a gravelly voice.

# INCARNATION

"I know what you've *done*," I replied, hoping I sounded more confident than I felt.

He threw his head back and chuckled — a harsh, grating noise that put me in mind of a manhole cover being dragged off the entry to a sewer line.

"Apparently my reputation precedes me," he said.

"Infamy is more like it," I shot back, then briefly wondered if I should be needling this guy with my snide remarks. He was an Incarnate, after all.

Nevertheless, if he was insulted by my comments, he didn't show it.

"You didn't heed my warning," he remarked.

I shrugged. "I'm on a superhero team. We get threats and warnings with our morning coffee. They're routine."

"Then how about something that's not routine," the killer proposed. "An offer."

I frowned. "What kind of offer?"

"Simply do as I requested before: stay out of my way."

"And what do I win if I play the game by your rules?"

Chuckling, the killer replied, "You mean besides your life? That's not incentive enough?"

"You've got the life of an Incarnate," I stated, "but you're running around killing folks. Obviously life, in and of itself, isn't enough."

The killer merely stared at me for a few seconds, then remarked, "You understand more than I gave you credit for."

I didn't say anything, merely stood there while he gave me an appraising stare. Basically, I had simply intended to keep him talking, hoping that he'd reveal something noteworthy, but apparently I had struck a nerve of some sort.

"Very well," he finally said. "Do as I ask, and we'll share in the power of the Incarnates."

# INCARNATION

## Chapter 38

The killer left immediately after making his offer, and it was truly instantaneous. One moment he was there, and the next, he — along with the roiling darkness — was gone, and my wall was back the way it had always been.

Wasting no time, I telepathically reached out for Rune, locating him in his quarters. Mentally, I told him to meet me in the living room of our suite immediately and then broke the connection. Eager to tell my story, I teleported to the rendezvous spot right away. Much to my surprise, Rune was already there waiting for me.

\*\*\*\*\*\*\*\*\*\*\*\*\*\*\*\*\*\*\*\*\*\*\*\*\*\*\*\*\*\*\*\*\*\*\*\*\*\*

Using telepathy, it took almost no time to bring Rune up to speed on what had happened. As soon as we were done, he insisted on seeing *where* it had happened. Thus, we ultimately ended up back in my bedroom, where Rune casually spun around once, his eyes raking over everything in sight.

"Okay," he said after visually taking in the place, "the first thing I'm going to say — and which is something I'm sure you know — is that the killer doesn't look like the visitor you had tonight."

"I know he didn't look like any of the Incarnates," I stated.

"Well, he'd have a tough time claiming innocence if he'd shown up sporting his *real* face."

"Seemed real enough to me."

"Hmmm," Rune droned. "That actually brings me to the second thing I wanted to say about your encounter with the killer: it didn't actually happen."

# INCARNATION

I stared at him in confusion for a moment, then blurted out, "What?"

"It wasn't real," Rune explained. "Looking around this room now, I don't see any indication that what you showed me telepathically truly took place here."

Stunned into silence, I simply gaped at him. I knew that Incarnates saw the world in a way that even *I* couldn't, but in this instance he had to be wrong.

"So what are you saying?" I asked. "That I just made it all up?"

"No," he insisted. "But I am saying that it was all in your head."

# INCARNATION

## Chapter 39

"Let me see if I've got this straight," I began. "You're saying that basically the killer created that entire scene that I saw in my *mind*?"

"Well, you did say you were sleeping just before it happened, right?" Rune asked.

"Yeah," I agreed with a nod.

"Trust me, it's nothing for an Incarnate to enter your mind — especially while you're asleep or dreaming — and create any illusion they want."

I let that sink in for a moment. We were back in the living room of our suite, where we had retreated while Rune offered his explanation of what had happened. He and I were now seated in our usual, respective positions on the easy chair and couch, discussing how events had likely unfolded. It went without saying, of course, that his explanation did not sit well with me. The notion of anyone — let alone a killer — running amok inside my mind had zero appeal to me.

"But when it was over, I was on my feet," I protested, "standing right where I'd been while he and I spoke."

Rune shrugged. "Maybe you sleepwalked through part of it. Maybe since your mind thought it was real, your body just reacted as it normally would. Or maybe…"

All of a sudden, he stopped speaking, as if something objectionable had occurred to him.

"Or maybe what?" I pressed, not letting him off the hook.

Rune looked pensive for a moment, then said, "Or maybe the killer took control to a certain extent, directing your actions so that the interaction you had was more real to you."

My eyes went wide in surprise. "He can do that?"

"Unfortunately," Rune muttered. "But we're big believers in free will, so it's not something Incarnates do as a matter of course."

"And this guy is a stickler for the rules, right?" I blurted out sarcastically, then groaned in agitation. "You know, just when I think this situation can't get any worse, it actually does. I mean, the last thing on my list of possibilities — even below getting killed — was the murderer getting in my head and puppeteering me."

Rune responded with a what-do-you-want-me-to-say expression.

"Are you sure that's what happened?" I pleaded, hoping for a different answer. "Not me being a puppet — I mean that entire conversation taking place in my head."

"Pretty much," Rune declared with a nod. "Aside from nothing in the room suggesting that it happened in the real world, I didn't detect the use of Incarnate power at the level necessary to create what you saw."

"Could it have escaped your notice?"

"Believe me, I would have felt it," Rune insisted. "But if it makes you feel better, we can get a second opinion."

# INCARNATION

## Chapter 40

"I concur with Rune," Endow said. "As far as I can tell, Jim, your encounter with the killer didn't take place in the real world — or, at least, not in your bedroom."

"Thanks," Rune said, then turned to me.

We were still in the living room of our suite. Endow, of course, was the second opinion Rune had suggested. He had reached out to her, and she had responded almost immediately, showing up within moments. Then, after telepathically being brought up to speed, she had inspected my bedroom and was now sitting on the couch a few feet from me, rendering her opinion.

"Anyway," Endow said, "I think we need to focus more on what was said during Jim's interaction with the killer rather than when and how it occurred."

"No need to build a think tank to figure that out," Rune noted. "The conversation boils down to one thing: the killer's not done."

"So what's next on his agenda?" she asked.

"I'd argue it's more of a *who's* next," I stated.

"Well, you're the detective," Rune reminded me. "Any leads in that department, Sherlock?"

I was about to answer in the negative, and then I remembered a subject that had gotten completely overshadowed by my encounter with the killer.

"Maybe," I said, leaning forward. "Let me ask the two of you something: have you ever heard the term 'mouses'?"

They both frowned, the word obviously sounding as odd to them as it did to me.

"You mean mice?" asked Endow, putting forth the obvious question.

I grimaced slightly. "Honestly, I don't know, but I don't think so."

"Where'd you hear that term?" Rune asked.

"Just came across it," I replied casually, hoping that Rune wouldn't delve further in that area.

"Well, if it's in reference to vermin," Endow offered, "we don't have any here. No mice, no flies, no rats…"

"You have vermin," I corrected. "He just walks upright, on two legs."

Neither of the two Incarnates responded to that, but I hadn't really expected them to.

"What about 'kleop'?" I continued. "Ever heard of that?"

Both Endow and Rune shook their heads.

"Where are you getting these words?" Rune asked.

"I thought I heard one of the *laamuffals* mention them," I replied, ingraining a bit of truth in my response. "I suppose it begs the question: what kind of education do those guys get?"

"Do you mean before or after they come into our service?" Endow asked.

I shrugged. "Both, I guess."

"We look for people who are pretty savvy," Rune offered. "You can't be stupid and do the job we require. Moreover, as we tend to seek out people with a certain level of curiosity, they usually continue to learn after they're with us."

"To be honest, though, it's self-education to a large degree," Endow added.

"Interesting," I muttered, but — not wanting to pique the curiosity of my two companions too much — I didn't say anything more.

# INCARNATION

"Well, if that's all for now, I think I'll be going," Endow said, coming to her feet. "I need to check on Ursula."

"I'm sorry," I intoned a bit sheepishly, and then stood up as well. "I didn't even ask: how is she?"

"Fine — practically back to her old self already," Endow replied with a smile. "All thanks to you, of course."

I found myself blushing slightly, struggling for something to say.

"Oh, that reminds me," I blurted out a moment later. Reaching into my pocket, I pulled out the stone prism that Ursula had made materialize earlier. "This belongs to Ursula."

"Ah," Endow droned in surprise. "*That's* what happened to it." Taking the object from me, she asked, "Do you know what this is?"

"No," I replied, shaking my head.

"It's a relic," she said. "After what happened in the room where Gamma died, I gave it to Ursula. It was supposed to protect her — specifically, from Reverb's voice if she were ever around when he spoke."

"Really? That was thoughtful of you to be mindful of her safety like that," I noted. As I spoke, I cast a steely glance at Rune, who somehow at that moment found something incredibly interesting on the floor to look at.

I turned back to Endow, saying, "Any idea why she wasn't wearing it at the time Reverb was attacked?"

"She said it clashed with her outfit," Endow answered, shaking her head in derision.

I laughed, and a moment later, Endow joined me.

"Anyway," I said a few seconds later, "at least she knew where to find it when she needed it, and I bet she'll have it handy next time."

"There won't *be* a next time," Rune interjected.

His comment, a sobering reminder that Reverb was gone, seemed to suck all the air out of the room.

"Here," Endow said, holding the relic back out to me. "Why don't you keep it — as a souvenir."

"Are you sure?" I asked, tentatively reaching for the prism.

"Of course," she declared. "And with Reverb gone, it's not like it's needed any more."

"Thanks," I mumbled, putting the prism back in my pocket. "Oh, one other thing before you go."

"Yes?" she murmured inquisitively.

"You mentioned earlier that *laamuffals* can engage in self-education," I reminded her. "What kind of resources do you guys have for that?"

"Well, with respect to Permovren, the castle has a library," she stated in a matter-of-fact tone. "Didn't anyone tell you?"

# INCARNATION

## Chapter 41

The information about the library was welcome news, and I was eager to get there. First, however, I felt the need for a more in-depth discussion with Rune.

Thus, almost immediately after Endow departed (vanished, to be honest), I turned to him and said, "Okay, why me?"

He gave me a blank look. "I don't understand the question."

"Why's the killer bothering with me?" I clarified. "I mean, it's just like you said before: back home my power set is considered impressive, but here — compared to Incarnates — it's nothing. *I'm* nothing. So again, why's he bothering with me?"

"First of all," Rune began, "that's not exactly what I said. Second, I think that we both know — even compared to Incarnates — you're far from nothing. More to the point, there's more to you than just your powers."

A bit embarrassed by the compliment, I made a noncommittal grunt in response.

"As to why the killer is interested in you," he continued, "I'd say it relates to the very fact that you're here."

I gave him a baffled look. "I don't think I follow."

"Your very presence here means that you're uniquely qualified in some way for the task you've undertaken. That being the case, the killer doesn't know how close you are to figuring things out — to being able to identify him."

"Oh yeah, I'm *real* close on that," I remarked sardonically. "About as close as Pluto to the sun."

"Well, the killer doesn't know that, so he's seemingly playing the odds."

I thought about it for a moment. "So essentially, what he's done is the equivalent of an indicted mobster trying to warn or buy off witnesses or the judge."

"Exactly."

"Of course, all of this presumes that *you* aren't the killer."

"Of course," Rune echoed in agreement.

"Hmmm," I droned, as a new thought occurred to me. "Doesn't it concern anyone that you're a suspect, and I as the investigator am essentially giving you the benefit of the doubt?"

Rune appeared contemplative for a moment, then said, "After Gamma's murder, it was up to one of us Incarnates to find someone to investigate. I mean, aside from not having the proper skills, there was an inherent conflict in having us investigate ourselves."

"One of you was — *is* — the murderer," I chimed in. "Wouldn't do to have the killer investigate his own crime."

"Bingo," he said with a nod. "Now, with respect to finding someone, I drew the short straw."

"And you selected me."

"Yes, for reasons we've already discussed. However, we all knew that whoever was brought in was going to have lots of questions — about Permovren, Incarnates, the murder, and so on. It was imperative that they be able to rely on the answers they were being given, which meant pairing them with someone they trusted."

"Which is how you ended up being my handler for this project," I concluded, "despite the fact that you're a suspect."

"Well, I'm not wild about the term 'handler,'" he stated, "but that's essentially it."

"Isn't anyone worried that I'll go easy on you?" I asked. "Cut you some slack because we're in the Alpha League together?"

"Would you?"

"No," I declared without hesitation. "Especially not if murder's involved."

"That's my point — that you're going to do the right thing. It's something all the Incarnates sensed about you."

I spent a moment considering that, then said, "But if you all sensed that about me, why is the killer basically offering me a bribe?"

"Because, like bad guys everywhere, he's assuming that deep down inside you're like him. That being the case, he's looking to exploit a vice he believes is fairly common."

"Which is what?" I asked.

"That everyone has a price," Rune said flatly.

# INCARNATION

## Chapter 42

After my conversation with Rune ended, I decided to spend a little time at the library researching the two words Cerek had written. Of course, I had no idea where it was located, but Rune was kind enough to simply transport me there with a wave of his hand.

I popped up in the middle of a cavernous room that seemed at least as wide as a city block. The place was populated primarily by elegant ten-foot-tall bookcases that were geometrically spaced throughout (and, as expected, filled with books). In addition to its breadth, the room rose up about four stories in height to a magnificent domed ceiling. Moreover, each floor above me was framed by an ornate wooden railing and looked out over the area in which I was currently located.

Apart from its size, one of the first things I noticed was that the room displayed a certain degree of opulence, starting with baroque architecture in the form of stately columns. There were also florid chandeliers that hung down from the ceiling, and all the furnishings — desks, tables, chairs, and more — appeared to be made of hand-carved wood. In a similar vein, the floor appeared to be comprised of marble tile. Finally, there was beautiful artwork everywhere — everything from paintings to sculptures to ceramics.

I stood there simply admiring the luxurious layout of the library for perhaps a minute after I arrived. I might have stood there longer, but for someone tapping me lightly on the shoulder from behind. Caught by surprise, I spun around and found myself facing a lady dressed in the garb of the castle servants.

# INCARNATION

I didn't know where she had come from — hadn't even seen or heard her approach — but didn't get any impression of menace from her. She was a handsome woman, maybe forty years old, with brown hair that came just short of reaching her shoulders. Smiling, she gestured toward a nearby desk and chair.

Taking the hint, I walked over to the desk and took a seat. In the meantime, the woman — whom I took to be a librarian of sorts — went to a nearby bookcase and pulled out a large, richly bound tome. Bringing it over, she placed it on the desk in front of me and walked away.

I stared at the book for a moment. It was oversized — approximately a foot-and-a-half in height and perhaps one foot wide. It was also markedly thick, and if I had to guess, I'd say it had at least a thousand pages. Maroon-brown in color, it was hardbound and made from some material I would be hard-pressed to identify. In addition, although it was untitled, it was covered with unusual designs and symbols embossed in gold.

In short, the book was stunningly beautiful, practically a work of art. Moreover, from all appearances, it struck me as being antiquarian, although I was nowhere near knowledgeable enough to guess its age.

I looked around for the librarian, suddenly curious as to why she had placed this particular tome in front of me. (My initial thought was that Rune had somehow reached out and given her instructions of some sort.) However, she had seemingly vanished as swiftly and silently as she had appeared.

With nothing else to do (and with the obvious course of action in front of me), I opened the book to the first page and got quite the surprise: it was blank.

# INCARNATION

Frowning, I swiftly leafed through the tome, haphazardly stopping here and there to look at random pages. They were *all* blank.

Letting the book fall open to its center, I leaned back, trying to make sense of the situation. Assuming the librarian knew why I was here (and to be honest, I wasn't sure that she did), why would she give me a blank book? For that matter, why would anyone make such a spectacular item and just leave it barren?

Of course, it was possible that someone had intended to write something on the pages by hand and had simply never gotten around to it. Or maybe the words were written in invisible ink or something. Or maybe...

I groaned in exasperation. There were quite a few reasons why the book might have — or appear to have — blank pages. At the moment, however, I wasn't sure if this book was even what I needed to help me figure out what Cerek's clues meant.

Now vexed, I reached out, preparing to close the book and seek some other way to do the necessary research. My hand froze just as I touched the tome and my mouth almost fell open. Shockingly, words were appearing on the page, and the first one — positioned on the page like a heading — was "MOUSES."

# INCARNATION

## Chapter 43

For all intents and purposes, the book essentially acted like a published version of an internet search. It focused on the topic at hand (which I presume it somehow extracted from my mind) and produced page after page of related information.

By my estimate, it took maybe fifteen minutes of reading through the book's references on "Mouses" to find the information I was looking for. When I did, I simply sat there in shock for a moment as the implications hit me. If I had truly figured out Cerek's clue (and I believed that I had), then I knew who the murderer was.

That said, there was still a chance that I was wrong. More to the point, if I *was* wrong, a misstep at this juncture would just tip the killer off. No, I needed to be absolutely certain I was right before pointing the finger at anyone in particular.

Unfortunately, there was no way to establish the facts with any degree of certainty — not without more information. And then I almost laughed out loud. I *had* more information.

Or rather, I had a way to *get* more information: Kleop — the other clue I had received from Cerek.

Still chuckling to myself regarding my blatant oversight, I stared at a blank page of the book and started focusing on the topic I had in mind. As before, words began forming, this time with "KLEOP" as the heading.

However, words had barely begun forming on the page before I felt something like a small tremor pass through the library, rattling furniture and bookcases to a small extent. Without being told, I knew what had happened.

# INCARNATION

A few moments later, Rune appeared, sporting a gravely serious expression. He merely looked at me, without saying anything. On my part, I simply gave him a nod, indicating I was ready. A second later, we vanished.

## Chapter 44

We popped up in what was probably a hallway on some blueprint of the castle, but it was hard to tell with the naked eye because the walls had been blasted to rubble for a hundred feet in every direction. It was obviously the handiwork of the killer, once again eliminating the possibility of the crime scene being reverse engineered.

I looked around to get a quick head count. In addition to Rune and myself, others present included Endow, Mariner, and Static. That meant...

"Pinion?" I said, directing my question at Rune.

"Yeah," Rune stated with a nod. "He's gone."

His words seemed to echo around us, sullen reminders not only of the fact that we'd lost someone else, but that the killer was still among us.

Now that the subject had been brought to mind, I glanced at the person I believed to be the murderer. The suspect looked no less troubled or concerned about Pinion's death than anyone else. However, that didn't necessarily mean anything. The killer had played the role of grieving friend through two prior deaths; it was probably old hat at this point.

"So, Rune, is the third time the charm?" Static asked, cutting into my thoughts. "Have we had enough deaths to convince you that we need the Kroten Yoso Va?"

"If we keep dying at this rate, we won't need it," Mariner noted. "The killer will be the last man standing."

"Regardless, I still say using it now would be premature," Rune shot back.

The conversation between the Incarnates then turned into a bickering session that was almost a repeat of the earlier discussion, with Static calling for use of the Kroten Yoso Va and Rune rebuffing his arguments.

Having heard this topic discussed previously, I tuned them out for the most part. Although I personally agreed with Static, I didn't like the idea of publicly opposing Rune on the subject (not to mention the fact that no one had asked my opinion), so I kept my thoughts to myself.

At that point, the squabbling came to a hard stop with Rune abruptly announcing, "This conversation's over."

Moments later, we were back in our suite.

# INCARNATION

## Chapter 45

We appeared in the living room. Rune, with a scowl etched on his features, was obviously still dwelling on the discussion he'd just had. Thinking he might want a few minutes to himself, I excused myself and was about to teleport to my apartment when he called out.

"Hey," he began, "I'm sorry you had to hear us quarreling like that."

"Not a big deal," I assured him. "However, I did have one question."

"Go for it," Rune said.

"Well, you guys keep talking about using the Kroten Yoso Va," I stated, "but you told me that you left it."

"I remember," Rune declared with a nod.

"But you also told me that nothing can get in or out of Permovren right now. So how exactly would you get it here?"

"The most straightforward way would be to eliminate the seal," Rune said.

I could almost have kicked myself. That was obviously the most direct method of getting the Kroten Yoso Va here, and I had completely overlooked it. Moreover, failing to consider that option had led to me asking what I now thought of as a boneheaded question.

"However, getting rid of the seal is the last thing I want to do," Rune continued. "Once that's gone, the murderer can get out."

"And then all bets are off," I said, remembering our prior chat about the difficulty in taking on an Incarnate with their full slate of powers. "So is there a way to bring it here without getting rid of the seal?"

"There is, but it's tricky," Rune stressed. "But as I keep saying, we're not there yet."

# INCARNATION

## Chapter 46

After finishing my conversation with Rune, I teleported to my quarters, popping up in the living room. I flopped down on the couch and then rubbed my temples for a moment, trying to relax.

Thinking about everything that had happened of late — especially the most recent murder — I found myself sighing gloomily. I hadn't known Pinion well, but that didn't mean I couldn't share in the grief I knew Rune had to be feeling, even if I couldn't detect it. In addition, I felt Pinion's demise weighing heavily on me, especially with it coming so close on the heels of Reverb's death.

Basically, I had been brought in to find a killer, but my progress in that department had been astonishingly slow. Now, as a result of my slothful pace, there had been not just one but two additional murders.

*Who am I kidding?* I thought. These were Incarnates getting knocked off. If they — with all the things they could do — couldn't save themselves or find the murderer, what chance did I have? Even if my research was accurate and my hunch about the killer's identity turned out to be true, would it do any good? I seriously doubted that, when the dust settled, I'd be able to save the Incarnates. I wouldn't even be able to save myself. I wouldn't be able to save anybody — not Rune, not Endow, not Ursula...

I sat up, blinking in surprise as I had a sudden epiphany: actually, there *was* somebody I could save. *Two* somebodies, to be exact.

Incredibly excited (and well aware of the fact that I was about to break some rules), I then cycled my vision to the appropriate portion of the spectrum and teleported.

# INCARNATION

\*\*\*\*\*\*↑↑↑↑\*⊹◦|◦|◦|◦\*↟↟↟\*\*\*\*\*\*\*\*\*\*\*\*\*

I popped up in the Cosmos Corridor. Much to my dismay, however, someone was already there: Static.

He was in the middle of the room, with his back to me. I couldn't quite see what he was doing, but got the impression that he was devoting single-minded focus to the task at hand. (I also couldn't see what I was looking for, and so assumed he was blocking my view.)

I immediately made myself invisible. Basically, I wasn't supposed to be there, and thus didn't like the notion of having to explain my presence. Then, I remembered: even when I was invisible, Incarnates still possessed the ability to see me. That being the case, my little plan appeared to be over before I even had a chance to effectuate it — especially when Static, perhaps detecting my presence in some fashion, glanced around for a moment.

Swiftly scanning the room, his eyes passed right over me. Feeling that my cover was blown, I was about to make some flimsy excuse about looking for Ursula when — seemingly satisfied — Static turned back to whatever he was working on. In short, he was apparently so preoccupied with his current endeavor that he hadn't noticed me. (Or, it suddenly occurred to me, maybe he had seen me but just didn't feel it was worth his time to address me — a notion which actually seemed fairly likely.)

A few moments later, Static vanished in typical Incarnate fashion — one second he was there; the next, he was gone. With my view of the room now unimpeded, it only took me a second to find what I was looking for: the beam of light with the two figures on it. Not knowing how big my window of opportunity was, I swiftly put my plan into motion.

I dashed to the area where the receptacle was kept — the one Endow had used to save the sportscar driver. Grabbing it, I then hustled to the beam of light, where I happily noted that the two figures were still present, although they had moved significantly closer to the dimensional rift.

Slightly nervous, I opened the container. As before, it contained rows of colorful gemstones, all giving off a soft glow. At that point, however, I abruptly realized that my plan was half-baked at best, because I had no idea what to do next.

In essence, I had planned to tear a page from Endow's playbook and use the gems to ensure that the guys on the light beam made it through the dimensional rift alive. The problem was that, although I had seen Endow use one of the gems, I honestly had no idea what they did or how they were differentiated.

Hoping that physical contact might convey some sense of the gems' properties, I picked a handful of them from the container and held them in my palm, eyeing them fiercely. Unfortunately, that garnered me no better indication of their attributes.

"Jim, is that you?" said an unexpected voice.

Caught with my hand in the cookie jar, my knee-jerk reaction was to hide the evidence. Thus, I made the gems in my palm invisible – at least to human sight. (With my vision cycled to another part of the spectrum, I could still see them.) At the same time, I looked around for the origin of the voice and saw Ursula standing near the entrance to the room.

# INCARNATION

"Come on, Jim," she droned as she approached. "I know it's you. I can see something seemingly floating in the air by itself, like when you displayed your powers before."

Taking my eyes off her for a second, I stretched out the hand holding the gems toward the figures on the shaft of light. Tilting my hand up, I curled my fingers over my palm so that they made a funnel of sorts. I then "poured" the gems out over the two forms on the light beam.

My intent was to split the number of gems evenly between the two figures. However, in my haste (or perhaps due to anxiety), I actually dropped a few more on one than the other. As with the driver Endow had gifted, the gems disappeared upon contact with the figures, and for a second I wondered if I should have thought about this more rather than acting on impulse. A moment later, however, Ursula was standing next to me and I had no more time to dwell on the subject.

Making myself visible, I said, "Hi. What are you doing here? I thought you were convalescing."

"My injuries weren't that severe and I made a quick recovery," she replied. "I'm here because I received notice of an unauthorized presence in the room."

"Notice?" I repeated in surprise.

She nodded. "Yeah, it's kind of like a silent alarm. Lets us know when unauthorized persons are in an area under Endow's purview — like this room. Now tell me, what are you—"

She stopped abruptly as she suddenly noticed what I was holding. Her eyes then shot to the beam of light, then back to the container and finally to my face.

"Oh, Jim," she almost moaned. "Please tell me you didn't try to do this."

# INCARNATION

I didn't say anything, merely looked at the ground forlornly.

"Jim!" she exclaimed, continuing. "You can't do that! Only Incarnates can bestow gifts."

"What did you expect?" I shot back. "I couldn't just let them die, and no one else was doing anything."

She gave me a sad, woeful look. "Look, I have to report this — tell Endow."

"I understand," I declared with a nod. "I'll deal with whatever punishment is appropriate, but I'm not sorry."

# INCARNATION

## Chapter 47

I teleported back to my quarters after the conversation with Ursula. I had probably burned some bridges with that little maneuver, but as I'd told Ursula, I wasn't sorry. It was something I had felt needed to be done (and in retrospect, I actually wished I'd done it earlier).

Now it was just a matter of when I'd be confronted about it. A few minutes later, Rune reached out telepathically.

<Something's come up,> he said. <You ready?>

<Sure,> I stated in resignation.

A moment later, I found myself back in the area where Pinion had been killed. It had not yet been repaired, and therefore still resembled a war zone to some extent.

As expected, all of the Incarnates were present, including my number-one suspect. At the thought of the killer, I spent a brief moment considering whether I should have devoted time to completing research on the clues Cerek had provided rather than trying to save the people in the Cosmos Corridor. However, my resolve quickly strengthened, with me concluding that — all things considered — I had made the right decision. Moreover, depending on how egregious they considered my conduct, I might still have a chance at walking away with a slap on the wrist.

"So, shall we get started?" I said to no one in particular, ready to get this over and done with.

"Of course," replied Endow. "Here's the gear."

"Gear?" I repeated, then noticed that she had her hand extended before her.

There, floating about three inches above her open palm, was a small metal cog. I immediately recognized it as the one that had previously resided on Pinion's hat.

"After Pinion's death," Endow explained, "I returned to my quarters and found this waiting for me."

"It appears that Pinion sent it there after he was attacked," Rune added.

My eyebrows went up in surprise — mostly due to the fact that we apparently were not here to parley about my recent antics. It seemed that Ursula hadn't ratted me out after all (or at least, not yet).

Wanting to keep the conversation on its present course, I said, "Why would he do that? I mean, I saw him use that gear as a weapon. Why would he get rid of it?"

"Because he was losing the fight," Mariner surmised, "and he didn't want it destroyed when the killer decimated this place."

As he finished speaking, Mariner made a gesture encompassing the surrounding rubble.

My brow furrowed as I focused on what I'd just heard, trying to discern the meaning. After a few moments, I thought I had it.

"If Pinion wanted to preserve the cog, that means it's a clue," I deduced.

"More than a clue," Static chimed in. "It's evidence. It can pinpoint the killer."

# INCARNATION

## Chapter 48

Like many metal surfaces, it turned out that the exterior of Pinion's gear was reflective. Although not exactly mirror quality, it did produce a likeness of things around it. More to the point, Incarnates apparently had the ability to extract past reflections from it.

In addition, the gear also had another unique attribute: it could, based on their powers, identify which individuals (i.e., Incarnates) were in close proximity or had used their *sivrrut* near it.

In short, it should be possible to use the gear to identify who was with Pinion when he died. However, the technique used to extract the information was going to be a little different than that used by the Incarnates to reverse engineer a crime scene.

"So what's next?" I asked after the others had explained the importance of Pinion's cog.

"One of us needs to work on the gear to extract the necessary information," Endow answered.

"I'll do it," Static volunteered. "I was hoping to do more to find my mother's killer."

"Very well," Endow said. No sooner had she stopped speaking than the gear floated from her hand to Static, who grabbed it.

"I'll need a bit of essence from everyone for comparative purposes," Static remarked.

Without a word, Rune and Mariner appeared to reach up and pluck a hair from their respective heads, while Endow took one from an eyebrow.

Noticing my confused expression, Rune explained, "It's kind of like a mystical DNA test. Each string of hair is infused with a portion of our essence. Static will compare that to what the gear contains to determine who was present when Pinion was killed."

I nodded, reflecting on the information that had just been presented to me. Assuming the test in question was reliable, it should adequately back up my supposition as to who the murderer was — or vice versa. Regardless, it appeared as though we were going to be able to identify the killer soon.

"You, as well," Static said to me, interrupting my thoughts.

"What?" I muttered, momentarily baffled.

"He's asking that you provide a sample, too," Endow clarified.

"I get that," I groused. "I just don't know *why*. Incarnates are the only suspects, and I don't even know if I have this 'essence' he's referring to."

"It's for exclusionary purposes only," Static insisted.

I shook my head. "I don't even know what that means."

"He wants to exclude you as the killer," Rune chimed it.

"Which takes us back to my earlier statement," I stressed. "Why am I even *in*cluded if the murderer is an Incarnate?"

"Just go with it," Rune said. "I'll explain later."

Still not happy with this turn of events, I plucked a hair from my head with my thumb and forefinger. A moment later, it began to glow with a gentle amber hue, as did the hairs from Rune, Mariner, and Endow. Following this, I felt a slight tugging on the hair, like someone trying to yank it from me.

# INCARNATION

I let it go; instead of falling to the floor, the hair went floating toward Static, as did everyone else's. Ultimately, he had five of them in front of him. (Presumably one was his own.) I kept a close watch on mine, namely because — if this were somehow going to be determinative of who the killer was — I didn't want there to be any confusion. (Speaking of the murderer, I kept my eye on my lead suspect, in case this turn of events caused them to do something untoward, but didn't note them doing anything unusual.)

Unexpectedly, something like a tiny glass case formed around each hair.

"The analysis will take a little while," Static said. "I'll let everyone know when I'm done."

And with that, he vanished.

# INCARNATION

## Chapter 49

"Okay, explain," I demanded. "Exactly what do I need to be excluded from?"

Rune and I, along with Endow, were back in our suite's living room, where he had just transported us following the recent discussion with the other Incarnates.

Rune seemed to ruminate for a moment, then said, "You know how Incarnates can pretty much be in two places at once?"

"Yeah," I conceded.

"And how we can present a false appearance?"

I nodded, thinking back to my encounter with the killer in my bedroom.

"Well," he continued, "bearing all that in mind, there's a possibility that on the occasions when the Incarnates met with you, it wasn't really *you*."

I concentrated, letting my brain digest that for a moment. "So you're saying that the murderer may have pretended to be me at some point, and Static wants to identify those instances when it was actually *me* who was present."

"Correct," Endow chimed in. "For instance, if Pinion's cog were to show your reflection at the time he was killed, but the essence identified at that time belonged to a *Chomarsus*—"

"It would mean that an Incarnate had pretended to be me," I interjected.

"That's it in a nutshell," Rune declared.

"But if something like that happened, wouldn't the rest of you be able to sense it?" I asked. "That is, each of you always seem to have a fix on where the others are. If the appearance changed but the essence stayed the same, wouldn't you know?"

"Not necessarily," Endow stated. "If I made a copy of myself but didn't want anyone to notice it, I might broadcast my power from the original so forcefully that it overshadows the second."

Seeing me wrestling with the concept, Rune said, "Think of it like the sun and moon being right next to each other. In that scenario, if you just look up during the day, you probably wouldn't be able to tell that there are two heavenly bodies there, because the light from one will completely overwhelm what you would see from the other."

"Okay, I can understand that," I said. "So is that why you guys can't figure out who was with Gamma and the others when they were killed? The murderer is somehow masking his trail, so to speak?"

"Basically," Endow conceded. "But to be clear, there are other methods that will accomplish the same result, and with our current limitations, even Incarnates can't watch for everything."

"We simply can't afford to spread ourselves that thin," Rune tacked on. "Trying to do too much can be as ineffective as doing too little."

"So let's forget about the murderer for a second," I said. "Let's talk about the victims — what happens to their *sivrrut* when they die?"

Rune and Endow exchanged a glance, then the former replied, "It dissipates. Goes back into the ether, void. Whatever you want to call it."

"So is there *no* way to pass a deceased Incarnate's power to someone else?" I asked.

# INCARNATION

"It just doesn't work like that," Rune stated. "As I mentioned before, our powers aren't like titles or possessions — they don't get bequeathed or passed on in the way you're suggesting."

"Hmmm," I droned, reflecting.

"What are you thinking?" Endow asked.

"I'm back to the question of motive," I said. "If the murderer somehow got the power of the deceased, that might explain the killing spree. But, since that doesn't seem likely, there's still the question of why."

"Any new leads on who's the likely culprit?" Rune inquired.

His question caught me a little flat-footed, as I hadn't planned to reveal the results of my research yet. After dawdling for a few seconds, I finally replied, saying, "Uh, not really. Also, if Static does the job right, it sounds like you won't need me anymore."

"Perhaps," Endow intoned.

"Speaking of Static," I remarked, "how do you know you can trust him?"

"You mean, what if he's the killer," Rune corrected. "Never fear. We plan to double-check his work. He has to know that, and so would be a fool to try anything crazy."

"If he *is* the killer, there's no doubt he's crazy," I countered. "That being the case, screwing around with some rinky-dink analysis doesn't even tip the scales when you're willing to murder Incarnates."

Endow looked as though she wanted to make a comment, but was cut off by Rune before she could utter a word.

"Heads-up," he said. "Looks like we have company."

# INCARNATION

At that moment, the doors to our suite opened (which, now that I thought about it, seemed to be a seldom occurrence). A few seconds later, Ursula walked in.

# INCARNATION

## Chapter 50

I struggled to keep from looking nervous. I had practically forgotten about the fact that Ursula was intent on ratting me out regarding what had happened in the Cosmos Corridor. Presumably Endow had been too busy, but Ursula — being the dedicated employee that she was — had tracked her down.

*If Mohammed won't come to the mountain...* I thought.

"Your little maneater's here," Rune said to Endow, who gave him a withering look.

"Well, it's not like I get a lot of opportunities," Ursula shot back, "so I can't afford to be demure and reserved when a cute guy comes along."

She glanced at me as she finished speaking, and I fought to keep my cheeks from turning red.

Rune laughed. "Ha! Nobody will ever accuse you of beating around the bush."

"Ignore him," Endow urged. "Now, did you need me for something?"

*Here it comes*, I said to myself.

"No," Ursula stated, shaking her head. "I just need to speak with Jim privately for a moment."

Her statement gave me something of a start; I had been all but certain that she was about to apprise everyone of my misdeeds. Her statement had also seemingly come as a surprise to Endow, who exchanged a worried glance with Rune.

"It's fine," Rune assured his colleague. "She's in good hands."

Endow didn't appear quite as confident as Rune, which made me wonder if there was a problem of some sort. Nevertheless, she didn't protest when Rune stated that the two of them would be back shortly, and then they disappeared.

# INCARNATION

## Chapter 51

We ended up sitting on the love seat, with me essentially waiting to hear what Ursula wanted to say.

"What, no kiss 'hello'?" she asked.

"Not just yet," I answered, snickering uneasily. "You said you wanted to talk."

"Yeah, but not about anything serious," she intoned.

I frowned. Ursula was undoubtedly a flirt, but I had garnered the impression that she knew how to walk the line between that and her official duties. Now it felt like she had gotten Rune and Endow to excuse themselves on a pretext. Even though she seemingly hadn't told Endow what I'd done, her actions didn't sit well with me.

"Maybe we should talk about what happened in the Cosmos Corridor," I suggested. "And what you're going to say to Endow about it."

"I'll say whatever you want me to say about it," she purred, reaching up to run a hand through my hair.

"What's wrong with you?" I demanded, grabbing her wrist.

Unsure of what was going on, I reached out for her empathically, trying to get a handle on why she was acting this way. To my surprise, her emotions were all over the place: love, anger, sadness, joy, fear, and so on. Even worse, there were so many of them — and all of equal intensity — that it was impossible for me to say which was dominant and therefore directing her actions.

Hoping for more insight, I tried reaching for her telepathically and, skimming the surface of her mind, received a shock that almost made me jump: in her mind, staring back at me, was a skeletal face with blotchy skin that I had seen once before.

The murderer.

Ursula let loose with something like a battle cry. At the same time, a glowing blade appeared in her free hand and she sliced at me with it.

I shifted into super speed, and it was as though someone hit a pause button on her: she froze in place, with blade in hand, mouth open, and a crazed look in her eye. I quickly stepped back, getting out of range of what appeared to be some kind of enchanted knife.

She was obviously under the control of the killer, and for some reason he had sent her here to deal with me.

As if my thoughts on the subject were her cue, I saw Ursula's jaw quiver slightly. Then, her eyes began to move in a herky-jerky fashion, while at the same time a sound like a scream — her battle cry — began emanating from her mouth. In short, her movements were accelerating to match my own.

<Rune!> I shouted out telepathically. <You need to get back here!>

I didn't receive any kind of acknowledgment — didn't know if he'd even heard me. However, I didn't devote too much time to thinking about it as Ursula stood and advanced on me with the glowing knife.

Seeing no reason to take a chance, I teleported the blade from her hand to the grain fields outside the castle. I was on the verge of mentally congratulating myself on that maneuver when the blade reappeared in her grip. Or maybe it was a different one. Truth be told, it didn't matter, but it reminded me that I wasn't really fighting an ordinary opponent. I was up against an Incarnate.

# INCARNATION

"Why couldn't you just stay out of the way?" I heard the killer ask from Ursula's throat.

"How do you know I didn't?" I retorted.

Rather than respond, Ursula tried to stab me. I stood my ground but phased, and she went sprawling as the blade passed through my insubstantial form.

"I've watched you," the murderer said, as Ursula turned toward me. "You've made not even the slightest attempt to comply with my request."

Before I could reply, Ursula flung up a hand, pointing her index finger at me. Instantly, a spout of flame shot out in my direction, and a second later, I was engulfed by a conflagration. Still phased, I wasn't harmed but noticed that I could feel some of the heat. It was a stark reminder that, given time, the killer could negate my phasing ability. I needed to find a way to end this without harming Ursula.

Teleporting behind her, I turned substantial and then swept her legs out from under her. However, showing incredible dexterity, she contorted herself while going to the ground and threw a punch that struck me in the side. It felt like a stick of dynamite had gone off next to my rib cage.

Pain exploded in my side, and I went flying across the room, flipping over a couch and then skidding along the floor — knocking around various pieces of furniture in the process — before snapping a couple of legs off an ornate table and coming to a halt. I groaned in pain for a moment, then shut off my pain receptors as I heard the patter of feet approaching, at the same time turning invisible.

A moment later, Ursula appeared, wild-eyed and screaming, holding the baby grand piano over her head. It was incredibly surreal and would probably have been hilarious were the situation not so serious.

She stared at the spot where I lay on the floor, but obviously didn't see me. I took advantage of the opportunity to teleport to the far side of the room and climb to my feet.

Vexed and frustrated, Ursula flung the piano into a nearby wall, where it let out a bevy of discordant notes upon impact before dropping to the floor as little more than kindling.

Snarling like an animal, she turned around and scanned the room, obviously looking for me. On my part, I floated up into the air, staying still and quiet while pondering how to end this without Ursula (or me) getting hurt. Fortunately, the decision was taken out of my hands moments later when the cavalry arrived.

Rune and Endow reappeared just as suddenly as they had vanished. However, they looked like they were frozen in place, and I instantly understood that they were not moving at super speed.

Ursula apparently realized it, too, because she charged at them, the glowing blade once again in her hand. I reached out telekinetically and tripped her. Moving at super speed, she went down hard and went tumbling along the floor, a jumble of arms and legs. However, she was still headed straight at Rune, so I phased him, letting her pass through him before she banged to a stop against a wet bar. Letting out an animalistic growl, she quickly scrambled to her feet.

By this time, Rune and Endow were starting to move, indicating that they were catching up to me and Ursula in terms of speed. Unexpectedly, Ursula let out a howl like a demon, and something on par with a whirlwind made of lightning appeared out of the blue and engulfed the two Incarnates. Spinning with frightening velocity, it flung furniture around like matchsticks while randomly shooting electrical bolts into the room.

Without warning, the whirlwind flew apart — shattered as if it were made of glass. At the same time, Rune came dashing out of what had been its center, heading toward Ursula like a torpedo.

"Don't hurt her!" Endow screamed in a voice that seemed loud enough to shake the walls.

It wasn't clear that Rune had heard her, but rather than ram Ursula (who, from appearances, was bracing herself for impact), he unexpectedly swerved, coming up behind her. Before she had a chance to react, he placed his hands on either side of her head.

Ursula's response was to let out a thunderous, earsplitting scream that seemed to go on forever but was probably no more than thirty seconds at the most. When she was done, her eyes rolled back in her head and she would have slumped to the floor, but Rune caught her. A moment later, Endow was next to him, checking on her *laamuffal* with maternal regard.

Turning to me, Rune asked, "You always have this effect on women?"

# INCARNATION

## Chapter 52

As had happened following Reverb's death, Endow took Ursula and vanished almost immediately. I then spent a moment telepathically showing Rune what had happened.

"Ursula was under the killer's control," I stated after bringing him up to speed.

"It was worse than that," Rune said. "That whirlwind she formed was a *Chomarsus* creation. The killer was sending his *sivrrut* through Ursula."

I frowned. "I thought only Incarnates could handle that level of power."

"That's right," Rune confirmed. "Without mincing words, she should be dead."

I reflected for a moment. "Maybe she had a relic she was using."

"Yeah, the proper relic could store an Incarnate's power and let someone use it," he agreed. "We'll have to check it out, but for now we'll assume that's the case."

"Hmmm," I muttered. "Assuming nothing like a relic is involved, how much power do you think our killer could direct through someone he was controlling?"

Rune shrugged. "I don't know. We don't really have a gauge for measuring *sivrrut*."

"But could he direct enough power to kill a *Chomarsus* through another person?"

"I doubt it," Rune replied. "It would be like getting electrocuted — it would fry a normal person." Then his eyes narrowed as he looked at me, and he said, "Why do you ask?"

"Because if he could use another person to kill an Incarnate, Static's analysis is going to be useless. It could have been anybody being sent by the murderer to do his dirty work."

"No," Rune countered. "It's still the Incarnate's power that's being used — even if it's through another person — and that's the essence that will be identified by Static."

"So it *is* still a useful analysis," I concluded.

"Absolutely," Rune said. "And now it's time to see *how* useful, so get your game face on."

# INCARNATION

## Chapter 53

We met up in a spacious room that had as its most notable feature an oversized executive table, which we all took a seat around. Unlike last time, the table was large enough for everyone to spread out a little. As a result, no one sat right next to anyone else, but the empty chairs were a grim reminder of those who were no longer with us.

As was previously the case, I sat at the head of the table. On the left side, a few chairs down, was Static; a few chairs away from him sat Mariner. Directly across from Mariner was Rune. At the moment, however, we were missing Endow, who — as best we knew — was still getting Ursula situated. Presumably she would take a seat between me and Rune, across from Static.

Truth be told, I felt odd sitting at the head of the table. We were really here to get information from Static, so by my account it should be him at the head rather than me. However, Rune had insisted that I take that particular spot, and I hadn't felt like arguing.

I looked around the table, trying not to appear anxious. In very short order, Endow would arrive, following which we were likely to unmask a killer. Wondering how the others felt, I reached out empathically. As always, I didn't pick up anything from Mariner or Rune, but Static was practically on pins and needles — nervous, anxious, eager, and more. (Of course, he purportedly knew the identity of the killer, so it was only natural that he was apprehensive.)

Finally, after what felt like a lifetime, Endow appeared.

"My apologies for being tardy," she said. "You may have heard that my *laamuffal* suffered from injuries, so I wanted to make sure she was being well cared for before I left."

"No problem," I assured her. "How is Ursula, by the way?"

"Funny you should ask," Endow replied. "She's going to be fine and is lucky that — physically — she only suffered some minor bumps and bruises. Mentally, however, she's in a bit of a whirlwind, so I reached out telepathically to help her. And there, on the surface of her mind, was a memory of you, Jim, in the Cosmos Corridor with my gemstone box."

There was silence for a moment, then Rune demanded, "Jim, is this true?"

I sighed and then, attempting to keep my head high, said, "Yes."

"What did you think you were doing?" Rune asked.

"Trying to save lives!" I retorted, then looked around at the rest of the table. "Look, my father and uncle aren't from my world — they came there from another dimension. From everything I was told, they were going to die because of some kind of anomaly. So, yes, I helped them. Because in case you haven't figured it out, if my father dies in that dimensional vortex, then I'm never born. And if I'm never born, then I can't help you find the murderer."

There was silence for a moment as my words seemed to sink in. And then Static spoke up.

"But," he began, "you *are* the murderer."

# INCARNATION

## Chapter 54

I gaped at Static, almost certain my mouth had fallen open. Assuming it had, I was so stunned that no words were coming out.

"What do you mean he's the murderer?" asked Rune, effectively reading my mind.

"I mean that I extracted his image from the gear as the person who was there when Pinion was murdered," Static explained. "There were no other images from that event, meaning that no one else was present."

I simply blinked, unable to believe what I was hearing. This was not going in any way, manner, or form the way I had envisioned (which basically consisted of Static naming the same person that I suspected as the killer).

"I also analyzed the essence of every person here," Static continued. "Again, his was the only one present at the murder."

"There has to be some mistake," Rune insisted. "Some mix-up."

Static shook his head. "No. I thought of that, considered that maybe I'd mixed up the sample of his essence with someone else's. So, just to make sure, I extracted information from Pinion's cog regarding each occasion when we had been in Pinion's presence. All of *us*" — he gestured toward himself and the other Incarnates — "had contact with Pinion thousands of times, so the gear's record for the essence of each of us goes back years — well before the murders began." He then pointed at me, saying, "On the other hand, the gear first records *his* essence *after* the murders started."

# INCARNATION

"So," Mariner surmised, "there's no confusing his sample with anyone else's because the record of his essence is significantly shorter than everyone else's."

"Correct," said Static.

"But it makes no sense," muttered Rune. "He had never even been here until after Gamma died, and he was with Endow's *laamuffal* when Reverb was murdered. How could he have killed them?"

"I'm not sure," Static admitted, shrugging, "but I suspect he's been under the control of an Incarnate who's the real mastermind behind this and who may not even be here at present. Also, I've heard rumors he can actually be in two places at once."

"Still, all of this is pure speculation," Rune announced.

"Well, we could just ask him," Static suggested. Turning to me, he said, "As you can tell, we've pretty much figured everything out. It will go easier on you if you simply confess."

For a moment, I didn't say anything. While the others had been speaking, my mind had been racing, trying to figure out how I had gotten into this situation.

There was no way I was the murderer, but if I were being honest, the issue with the killer being in my head on that one occasion had really thrown me for a loop. Was it possible that I had done things unwittingly and unwillingly? That I was someone's puppet? It certainly wasn't *im*possible, but it was damned unlikely in my opinion — even if it was an Incarnate pulling the strings. Something was wrong here.

I reached out empathically, trying to see if anyone present was buying Static's story. As before, I couldn't pick up on any emotions besides those of Static himself, whom

I sensed was incredibly anxious, although he wasn't showing it physically.

"It's okay," he said again. "You can tell us what happened — confess to what you did."

As odd as it seemed, there actually was a little part of me that wanted to do as he asked. It was like there was a small voice in the back of my head telling me to own up to all these horrible things. I ignored it and tried to focus on some kind of rebuttal I could make, but the emotions Static was broadcasting was making it difficult, as he seemed to be on the verge of panic.

But why would a *Chomarsus* be nervous? What would an Incarnate panic about? Even with a murderer on the loose and targeting them, they had seemingly maintained their cool.

"Just confess," Static said again. "We know what you did. We've got the analysis, and it tells us everything."

I found myself getting angry. He could take his analysis and shove it! Bearing in mind what Rune had said about him being lazy, it was probably unreliable anyway. He probably took all kinds of shortcuts and...

My thoughts trailed off as the veil lifted and I had a clear understanding now of what had happened.

I turned to Static with a smile and said, "It's not *me* who needs to confess; it's *you*. You're the murderer."

# INCARNATION

## Chapter 55

Static went bug-eyed at my accusation, muttering, "W-w-what?"

"I've intentionally sat here quietly while you talked," I stated boldly, "letting you uncoil just enough rope to hang yourself — which you've done, thank you kindly."

"W-what are you talking about?" he muttered.

"I'm talking about the analysis of Pinion's gear," I replied. "You never did it."

"Of course I did!" he retorted. "Of course I did the analysis!"

I shook my head solemnly. "No, you didn't. You're inept, lazy, and prone to taking shortcuts. You never had any intention of performing that analysis because *you're* the killer. You already knew who was innocent, so why waste time doing a bunch of work trying to 'figure out' who did it? Your only goal was to control the process so you could find someone to frame."

"Lies!" Static screamed, now getting furious. "These are nothing but vicious lies! You're simply trying to avoid being punished for your crimes, but the evidence doesn't lie."

"There is no evidence," I shot back. "You never did the analysis."

"I did," he insisted, "and it shows you as the murderer. Your own essence is the evidence that convicts you."

"The evidence can't do any of that," I argued, "because I switched it."

"What??!!" shouted Rune and Mariner, almost in unison.

"I switched it," I said again. "Mine and Endow's, to be precise — with her permission, of course."

Static shook his head. "That's not possible."

"Sure it is," I countered. "I'm a teleporter."

As a demonstration, I then teleported to a corner of the room, then back to my chair.

"So," I continued, "I swapped my essence with that of Endow. Thus, if you had actually done the analysis you claim you did, it would have showed that I had interaction with Pinion going back years, while Endow only recently met him."

"N-n-no," Static muttered. "I don't believe you."

"Don't take my word for it," I stressed. "Ask Endow."

We both turned to Endow, who was in the midst of giving me an appraising glance. I was hoping she would back my play, and then it hit me.

*Endow can't lie!* I recalled.

Internally I groaned, thinking I had just spun an amazing yarn for nothing. Endow would tell him the truth, and Static would go back to his story.

Endow turned to Static and stared at him for a moment, then said, "Well?"

Static looked like a trapped animal and was breathing heavily and fast — almost hyperventilating. It was clear that the conversation had gone in a direction he had not intended.

Reaching out for him emotionally, I felt his panic swiftly dissolving, replaced by something hard, concrete, resolute...and menacing.

My eyes went wide and I tried to shout a warning to Rune, Mariner, and Endow. Before I could, however, something like a minor explosion seemed to take place within Static's body — a flash of light, accompanied by flesh seeming to flee his frame of its own accord. When I looked again, Static was gone, and in his place was a cadaverous form with blotchy skin and a skeletal face.

The killer.

# INCARNATION

## Chapter 56

Everyone seemed to go into motion at once, leaping to their feet and knocking their respective chairs over backward (including me). Shifting into super speed — which, frankly, everyone in the room seemed to do — I noticed that Mariner already had his flaming water-sword in hand, Endow wielded what looked like a medieval mace, and Rune had glowing spheres around his hands.

Static (whom we all now knew was the killer) didn't have a weapon. Instead, he raised a hand above his head; almost immediately, a brilliant white light flashed from something he seemingly held. When it diminished a few seconds later, I noticed two things right away.

First, the room had expanded notably in size. Whereas before it was perhaps twenty-by-twenty feet in size, it was now at least twice that, with everyone much farther spaced out than they'd been before.

The second thing I noticed (and which had me almost staring in shock) was that there were now two Runes, two Endows, and two Mariners.

Although dressed the same as the original Incarnates (as well as having identical appearances), the three newcomers were easy to distinguish because they weren't brandishing weapons of any sort. In addition, they appeared slack-faced and blank-eyed, as if no thoughts were going on in their brains.

As I sized up the new arrivals, a weird clacking noise reached my ears, almost a rattle of some sort. It took me a moment to realize what it was: Static laughing.

Without preamble, Static stopped his weird cackling and shouted, "Attack!"

# INCARNATION

At his command, the three newcomers abruptly launched themselves, respectively, at the original versions of themselves, wielding the same types of weapons (which had seemingly come from nowhere).

"And as for you..." he growled, looking in my direction.

I didn't wait for him to finish his statement, threat, comment — whatever he was going to say; I telekinetically grabbed the chair he'd been sitting in (which had tipped over when he'd gone to his feet) and shoved it forcefully into the back of his knees. Arms pinwheeling, he toppled over backward. As he went down, his head hit the floor with a sound like a cinderblock being dropped on concrete. Afterward, he lay there, moaning and dazed.

I took a moment to glance at the three Incarnates, and immediately realized that they were fighting for their lives. Their doubles were not only their equals in terms of appearance, it seemed, but also with respect to martial ability, weapon skills, and power.

I turned back to Static, who was still on the floor. Teleporting next to him, I reached down and tried to take the item he held in his hand — what he'd used to summon the doubles of Rune and the others. From all appearances, it appeared to be a green crystal about eight inches long — presumably some type of relic.

As I reached for it, his free hand suddenly snaked out and grabbed my wrist. Before I could react, he whipped his arm back and forth, slamming me to the floor in side-to-side fashion on either side of him. He then twirled me around once like a sack of leaves before flinging me into a nearby wall. I slammed into it hard enough to see stars and then slid to the floor.

# INCARNATION

Needless to say, I ached all over and immediately began shutting off the pain. Static might look like a frail bag of bones, but he was apparently as strong as a giant. More concerning than his strength, however, was something I had noticed while he was treating me like a towel that he was trying to swat bugs with: I had attempted to become insubstantial, but it hadn't worked. He was negating my phasing ability.

While this was going through my brain, I saw Static rise up. However, he didn't come to his feet like a normal person — that is, getting their legs under them, extending, and so on. Instead, he simply rose up the way vampires occasionally do in movies, with his body straight and rigid like a plank of wood.

Looking in my direction, Static snarled, and I expected him to charge at me. Unfortunately, despite much recent experience, I still had a terrible habit of underestimating Incarnates. Static didn't charge; he just disappeared and then reappeared right next to me before walloping me with a backhand. I went somersaulting through the air, but managed to halt my momentum after about twenty feet and then just floated.

For a moment, we just stared at each other, and then I flew at him, hard and fast. Watching me approach, I saw Static bracing himself, noting that I was coming at him at about chest height. However, just before I reached him, I turned invisible and went low, targeting his knees.

The impact was like hitting two stone pillars, but achieved the desired effect: his legs went out from under him, causing Static to do a solid faceplant on the floor.

Upon turning invisible, my vision had automatically switched to infrared. I now cycled it through the spectrum to something approaching normal and looked around.

Static lay on the floor, moaning in pain, but I wasn't going to be caught twice by a dazed-and-confused act. This time, keeping out of arm's reach, I simply teleported the crystal from his hand to mine. I then glanced at Endow and the others to see how they were faring.

Mariner appeared to be injured, with one arm hanging limp, while Rune took shelter behind a protective sphere as his double fired pulses of white light at him. Endow was retreating before a furious onslaught from her look-alike, who wielded her mace like it was part of her body. Things were not looking good for the home team.

I stared at the crystal, trying to figure out how to turn the thing "off." Unfortunately, it didn't come with a switch or a manual, so I found myself at a loss concerning what to do.

As I looked the crystal over, I noted Static rising to his feet again in the same eerie manner as before. This time, however, as I turned my attention to him, I also saw something that I hadn't previously noticed: Static was wearing a necklace with something like an amulet attached to it.

I hadn't seen it before, so he presumably had kept it tucked down the front of his tunic. Looking at it now, I realized what must have happened: as Static had been headed face-first to the floor, with his legs up and head down, the amulet had slid out from its usual spot. With him back on his feet, it now rested on the outside of his tunic.

Trying to get my head back in the game, I made the crystal invisible (like the rest of me) and continued inspecting it for a moment before temporarily giving up.

# INCARNATION

Turning my attention back to Static, I saw him spin around in a circle, obviously looking for the crystal I'd taken. I was mentally congratulating myself on outsmarting him when he suddenly vanished and appeared next to me. Faster than I would have thought possible, he reached out and gripped the wrist of the hand holding the crystal.

"Bad move, boy," he hissed. "The crystal is infused with my power — I know where it is at all times."

He snapped his fingers, and something like red dust seemed to pour over me from the ceiling. I knew without even thinking about it that I was now visible — and if I needed proof, I got it when Static placed his free hand unerringly around my throat and lifted me off the ground. Then he began to squeeze.

"You should have taken my offer," he said. "We could have both had the power of Incarnates."

As he spoke, I gripped the wrist of the hand around my throat, trying to pull it off. Because I'd already clamped down on the nerve endings, I wasn't feeling any pain, but that didn't mean Static wasn't doing any damage. For instance, I could feel my air getting cut off. Pain or not, that was a problem, because without air I'd pass out, and then it would be *lights* out.

Somewhat frantic, I teleported, hoping to get away from him. Shockingly, when I popped up about twenty feet away, he was with me, hand still around my throat and holding me aloft. Somehow, he had teleported with me.

Static laughed gleefully. "There's no escape — for you *or* your friends."

He tilted his head toward Mariner and the others, who were all fighting back-to-back now and looking exhausted. It was pretty clear that they wouldn't last much longer. Truth be told, neither would I, as evidenced by the

212

fact that I was already starting to see spots in front of my eyes. Even worse, I was beginning to hallucinate, because I saw something like a will-o'-the-wisp seep fervently out of the amulet around Static's neck.

In desperation, I tried to duplicate myself — make a second Jim who could perhaps take my adversary unawares from behind. Nothing happened; presumably, that ability was being blocked along with others.

With nothing to lose, I raised my dangling legs and kicked out as hard as I could toward Static's face. I connected and his head snapped to the side, but his hold on my throat only loosened slightly. However, it was enough for me to draw in a shallow breath before he reasserted his grip.

With the small gasp of air I was able to take in, the spots receded from my vision for a moment but the will-o'-the-wisp was still there. It snaked down and around, coming up behind Static where it swiftly began taking on a form I was familiar with: Cerek. However, he wasn't alone; with him was someone else I recognized — Reverb.

That said, Reverb was in terrible shape, to put it mildly. He had no arms or legs, and his torso was bruised and bloody. One eye was black and swollen shut, and one ear gave the impression of having been shorn off. The only thing on him that didn't look battered was the metal mask, which was still in place. Bearing in mind the extent of his injuries, I wasn't shocked by the fact that Reverb didn't appear to be conscious — he barely appeared to be alive — and was being held aloft by Cerek, who didn't look that great himself. Whereas before the *laamuffal* had seemed scraggly and scruffy, he now appeared completely frazzled.

I took all of this in within seconds. Not wanting to telegraph the presence of the new arrivals, I planted my eyes firmly on Static, but I could have saved myself the trouble. He was so intent on choking me out that he didn't even notice what was going on around him.

As before, Cerek seemed to be trying to tell me something. Sparing him a quick glance, I noticed him gesturing and then caught on. Assuming I understood him correctly, there was a slim chance of overcoming Static. It would be unbelievably risky and exceedingly dangerous — I couldn't bank on surviving — but it might buy time for Rune and the others.

I concentrated, and then teleported the metal mask off Reverb, sending it to a far corner of the room. Without the mask to support it, Reverb's mouth fell open, and an impossibly excruciating, agonizing sound issued forth.

# INCARNATION

## Chapter 57

Bellowing in pain, Static released me and collapsed to his knees, at the same time putting his hands up to cover his ears. I hit the floor and flopped onto my rear — not so much because Static had dropped me but because the entire room was shaking as a result of Reverb's voice. I floated up into the air, thereby managing to escape the tremors that were rattling everything in sight.

For a brief moment, I wondered how badly I was injured. (Again, just because my pain receptors were shut off didn't mean I wasn't getting hurt.) Simply eyeballing myself externally, it didn't seem like anything was out of joint. What's more, I was surprised to discover that I was still holding Static's relic — the one that had summoned the doubles of the Incarnates.

All of a sudden, the room stopped shaking. At the same time, I began to hear a queer sound, like someone sucking in air through a straw. I looked in the direction of the noise and realized it was Reverb drawing in breath. He was going to speak again.

Apparently Static realized the same thing, because he staggered to his feet unexpectedly and began mumbling, "No, no, no!"

Reverb's voice sounded again and Static went down to his knees for a second time, letting out an agonized howl as the room seemed to convulse. Taking advantage of the short reprieve, I looked toward Endow and the others but couldn't get a sense of how things were going due to the way the room was shaking (although they all still appeared to be on their feet). Regardless, we needed to bring the current conflict to a halt. I turned my attention back to Static's relic, hoping for a clue, but nothing revealed itself.

Moments later, the shaking stopped, only to be replaced by the air-through-a-straw sound again. Static, however, seeing his own window of opportunity, waved a hand in the general direction of Reverb and Cerek (who was still holding up the wounded *Chomarsus*), at which point two things happened. First, Reverb's mask suddenly appeared back in place, obstructing his inhalation of air. The second thing that happened was that both Reverb and Cerek went flying to the side, as if struck by a giant, invisible hand, eventually crashing into — and smashing through — one of the walls with bone-jarring force.

Breathing heavily, Static turned in my direction. Like Ursula previously, he had blood running from his ears, but he didn't seem to notice.

"You," he sneered, scowling at me. "*You* did this."

I didn't need any guesses to figure out that he was referring to Reverb's recent assault on him. Rather than respond, however, I teleported — popping up back in the living room of my quarters. It was an effort to buy time and perhaps figure something out.

Unfortunately, it turned out to be an exercise in futility, as I had been there barely a second before Static appeared as well. He popped up right next to me, and before I could react, he had his hand around my throat again. I beat at it ineffectually — even tried stabbing it with his relic — but my struggles barely registered with him.

Instinctively, I tried teleporting again — this time popping up in the room with the frescos. As before, however, Static came with me. It was as if direct contact made him a part of me, such that he went wherever I did.

(And if he noticed the change in our environs, he didn't show it).

"How are you alive?" he demanded, leaning in close. "Reverb's voice should have killed you." His eyes narrowed, and then seemed to light up a moment later. "Of course — you have something."

I didn't say anything, just continued striving in vain to get away. Static, ignoring my efforts, raised his free hand, which began glowing with an amber light. At the same time, I felt something getting warm near my leg, as well as my chest.

"Ah," Static muttered after a few seconds.

I felt the equivalent of a forceful tug near the pocket of my pants, accompanied by the distinct sound of fabric being ripped. A moment later, the souvenir Endow had given me — the prism-shaped relic that would offer protection against Reverb's voice — flew into Static's hand.

He stared at it for a moment, then said, "Impressive. Powerful. This one will make a fine addition to my collection. Which reminds me..."

Trailing off, he turned his eyes to my hand — the one that still held his relic — and the crystal was abruptly snatched from me by an unseen force. It went floating to his hand, joining the one he'd taken from my pocket. He then held the two items to his chest — specifically, he pressed them against the amulet he wore. Surprisingly, when he pulled his hand away, they stayed fixed to the talisman as if attached to it with superglue.

Noting my attention, he grinned.

"My growing collection," he explained, gesturing toward the relics and amulets. "Many thanks for your contribution. And don't worry — I'll take excellent care of it. It's in good hands."

I frowned as Static finished speaking. There was something about his words… Something about what he'd just said resonated with me, echoed in my head. It triggered a cavalcade of thoughts, memories… But they were jumbled, like pieces of a puzzle. I knew they fit together, but wasn't sure how. Even worse, considering my current situation, I didn't have much time to figure it out.

"What's this?" Static asked quizzically, bringing me back to myself. I noticed then that his hand was once more encased in the amber light, and my chest was getting warm again.

"You've got something else," he continued.

And with that, it came to me — all the pieces of the puzzle slid into place.

I reached for the badge that Rune had previously given me, which was the source of the heat I was feeling. Static, however, got to it first, pulling it from the interior of my shirt.

"Don't touch that!" I screeched, giving him an angry look. "It's mine!"

As if to emphasize my claim, I reached toward my neck and grabbed a portion of the badge's chain.

"Let go!" I roared. "It's mine! Mine, mine, mine!"

"No, it's *mine*," Static said calmly.

He then yanked on the badge, hard, snapping the chain that attached it around my neck. As he pulled it away, the portion of its chain that I held in my hand slithered through my palm like a wriggling eel.

"No!" I wailed.

Static gave me a smug look. "Very generous of you to add more to my collection before you die." He then began to squeeze my throat. "It's too bad you won't be around to see all the things I'm going to do, but I thank you."

"No," I croaked, smiling. "Thank...*you*."

Realizing all of a sudden that something was amiss, Static stopped attempting to throttle me. He simply looked at me for a moment, then stared at the badge with a frightening intensity. A moment later, his mouth fell open in horror, and he dropped both me and the badge.

"It can't be..." he mumbled, slowly shuffling backward, but never taking his eyes off the badge. "It can't."

"But it is," I assured him.

"No," he uttered, but without any confidence. At the same time, the badge began emanating a lavender light that appeared to pulse softly.

Seeing this, Static looked at me and pleaded, "*Please*. Take it back. You *have* to take it back."

"It's too late," I said as the light from the badge began to pulse faster. "It's done."

"No, wait!" Static begged as the pulsing light increased in tempo. "I'll do anything! Anything! I'll—"

His words were cut off as the light stopped pulsing and became steady — and then flared up with a brilliance and luminosity that was too intense to look at and which seemingly encompassed the entire room.

# INCARNATION

## Chapter 58

When the light receded, Static lay on the floor, curled up in a ball. He wasn't unconscious, but he was obviously addled, because he kept mumbling — making what appeared to be random, disjointed statements. Occasionally there would be an outburst from him, prompting me to do what I could to calm him down (which included skimming the surface of his mind to see what the problem was).

To be honest, I sensed that he was no longer a danger, but decided to get anything he might find useful out of his reach. With that in mind, I teleported my badge, his amulet, and the two relics into my hand for the nonce. Beyond that, I simply waited for someone to come take charge of him. (I suppose I could have teleported him, but didn't want to deal with the aftermath if a sudden change in scenery did something to his already-altered mental state).

Eventually, Mariner showed up. After seeing him looking like a winged bird earlier, I would have expected him to have his arm in a sling, but he appeared to be completely able-bodied. (Obviously, I kept forgetting how tough Incarnates were, such as when he had taken a knife in the eye.)

I left Static in his care, along with the crystal relic and amulet. Keeping my badge and the prism with me, I then teleported back to my quarters, at which point I immediately flung myself into the shower. After the lavender light had vanished, I'd found myself no longer covered in the red dust Static had dumped on me, but I'd still felt foul. A long shower went a long way toward making me feel clean. Afterward, I got dressed and then stretched out on the bed and got some much-needed sleep.

\*\*\*\*\*\*\*\*\*\*\*\*\*\*\*\*\*\*\*\*\*\*\*\*\*\*\*\*\*\*\*\*\*\*\*\*\*

I awoke feeling incredibly refreshed. Bearing in mind that physical needs were at a minimum in Permovren, it was pretty clear that the rest I'd gotten had benefited me mostly on a psychological level. (Apparently rooting a killer out of your midst does wonders for your mental health, including allowing you to sleep like a baby.)

Nevertheless, although the murderer had been caught and the threat eliminated, I still had some lingering questions. That being the case, I decided to finish up my research in the castle library.

Once there (and with the librarian's assistance once again), I was easily able to pick up where I'd previously left off. From that point, it didn't take me long to find the information I was looking for. However, I'd barely finished (and had almost no time to reflect on what I'd learned) when Rune and Endow showed up looking for me, saying that we needed to talk.

## Chapter 59

We ended up in a sitting room in Endow's chambers, probably because it seemed to be an area designed for three-person conversations, with a trio of exquisitely comfortable easy chairs arranged around a triangular table.

"So," I began after everyone had taken a seat, "is this the official debrief?"

"Not exactly," Rune said. "There are still a lot of unanswered questions about what happened here. At the moment, each of us three probably has a piece of the puzzle, but if we put them together we can probably see the big picture."

"Okay," I droned. "But what pieces are we talking about?"

"To begin with," Endow noted, "there's the information that you've gleaned from investigating the murders. Then there's what I've gathered from talking to Ursula, and what Rune has been able to get from Reverb."

"Ursula and Reverb?" I repeated quizzically. "What's their connection? Aside from being mind-controlled and almost killed, that is."

"I don't think Static realized Ursula has a telepathic ability," Endow said. "So, when he took control of her body, even though she couldn't do anything physically, she was able to see what was in his mind."

My brow furrowed as I contemplated that. "So she saw everything that happened when she attacked me?"

Endow nodded. "She saw it. She just couldn't do anything about it."

"But the real takeaway there," Rune insisted, "is that she was able to get some things out of Static's head without him knowing she was there."

"And Reverb?" I asked.

"He spent fair amount of time with Cerek," Rune stated, "who had a treasure trove of background information."

"Yeah, but how's Reverb even alive?" I asked. "I thought his effigy crumbled."

Endow sighed. "It's complicated. But maybe we should just start at the beginning."

"First though," Rune chimed in, "let me say that you did great, Jim. It's not everyone who would have been willing to take on an Incarnate, let alone beat him one-on-one."

"Except Static's not an Incarnate," I countered. "He never was."

Rune and Endow exchanged a glance, and then the latter asked, "When did you figure that out?"

"Not soon enough," I replied, "although I got enough hints."

Endow gave me an inquisitive look. "Like what?"

"For starters, all of the contrasts between him and the rest of you Incarnates," I stated. "For instance, I could always read him emotionally, but not the rest of you. When I was invisible, he didn't seem to be able to see me, but the other Incarnates could. And then, there was the fact that he mentioned being roused."

Endow frowned. "What's the significance of that?"

"Because for normal people, sleep is generally a necessity," I explained. "Even in a place like Permovren, where your body doesn't require it. We need the break, the ability to recharge our mental batteries." I paused for a moment to let that sink in, then asked, "Didn't you guys notice that he slept more than the average *Chomarsus*?"

"He did have a history of sleeping relatively often," Endow admitted.

"I just thought it was related to the fact that he was incredibly lazy," Rune added.

"Anyway," I said sheepishly, "I'm sorry I didn't pick up on those things sooner. Looking back on it, even his name was a giveaway: aside from referring to a type of electrical charge, 'static' also refers to something that's fixed or doesn't change."

"Gamma gave him that moniker," Endow noted. "In her own way, I guess she was telling us that he hadn't become an Incarnate."

I groaned in frustration. "I can't believe I was so slow in putting all that together."

"Don't blame yourself for that," Rune insisted. "We spent ages around him and never picked up on it. The fact that you homed in on it during a much shorter period is a credit to you."

"Well, he didn't pull this farce off on his own," I said. "He had a *real* Incarnate helping him most of the time."

"Gamma," Endow uttered. "It all started with her. We should have realized what she was capable of."

"Don't be angry with her," Rune said to Endow. "She just couldn't watch any more of her children die." He then turned to me, saying, "If you know that Static wasn't really an Incarnate, then you probably know what Gamma did."

I nodded. "Cerek told me — she shared her *sivrrut* with her son."

Endow looked at me in surprise. "You spoke to Cerek?"

"Sort of," I replied, making a waffling motion with my hand. I then proceeded to tell them about my two initial interactions with Gamma's *laamuffal*. They listened dutifully and without comment, although I did notice them share a look when I mentioned going into the fresco.

"So he left you clues on a bathroom mirror," Rune summed up when I finished. "How very *noir* of him."

"Well, you did lay this out as a murder mystery," I reminded him. "Sometimes life really does imitate art."

"So it seems," Rune stated. "Anyway, you're saying the two clues that Cerek gave you told you that Gamma was sharing her power with her son?"

"They told me that, as well as a few other things," I clarified.

Rune looked as though he had further commentary, but Endow cut him off.

"But I don't understand," she interjected. "Why wouldn't Cerek just come to one of us Incarnates? We'd have actually been able to talk to him in his astral form and would have been able to stop all this carnage."

"I think he was acting out of loyalty to Gamma," I said. "He was still trying to save her son."

"How?" Endow asked.

"Hold on," Rune chimed in. "We're hopscotching around a bit. It might be better if we try to take this in order."

"Fine with me," I declared. "We were talking about Gamma sharing power with her son."

"Yes," Endow said. "She'd already outlived a number of her children. Static was her youngest, and she couldn't bear the notion of seeing him grow old and die."

"So she cooked up a scheme where she shared her power with him — put half of it at his disposal — but told all of us that he was an Incarnate," Rune added.

"But couldn't you guys sense that her power had diminished?" I asked. "Couldn't you tell it had been chopped in half?"

"There's no yardstick for measuring *sivrrut*," Rune protested. "And as long as she had enough to carry out her duties, nobody cared."

"But surely there's some way to gauge it," I opined.

"I know it seems that way," Endow said, "but the scope of your question is broader than you think."

"How so?" I asked.

"Think of it this way," Rune interjected. "Imagine that I'm going to live forever, but I can give you half of my lifespan. How long is that? What's half of infinity? Because that's what your question boils down to with respect to Gamma sharing her power."

My brow furrowed as I mentally chewed on that. It certainly explained no one noticing any decline in Gamma's *sivrrut*. (And was also a testament to just how powerful Incarnates truly were.)

"Okay," I finally said. "I can understand why it would be difficult for you guys to notice that Gamma only had half a tank of gas. Of course, if she didn't want to see him die, she could have just piggybacked on the analogy Rune just gave and made him live forever."

"According to what Ursula got from him," Endow stated, "that wouldn't have been enough. He wanted *power* as well."

Her words brought to mind the conversation I'd had with Static the first time he'd appeared to me as the killer.

# INCARNATION

"Life, in and of itself, isn't enough," I said, reflecting.

Rune nodded. "Correct. So he throws a hissy fit about wanting power and Mom decides to calm him down by giving him what he wants, only she can't do it directly."

Rune pointed at the table between our three chairs and out of nowhere Static's amulet appeared on it, along with his crystal.

"She uses *this*," Rune declared as he reached out and grabbed the amulet. "It's a relic that can hold an Incarnate's power, and Gamma puts half of hers into it, thereby giving Static access to her *sivrrut*."

"Only it's still not enough for him," I added. "Static doesn't just want *access* to power. He wants it as his own. Somehow he accomplishes it, but I have no idea how."

Endow and Rune exchanged a glance, and then the former said, "He performed a...rite, of sorts. It bonded him to the relic containing Gamma's *sivrrut*, making it part of him and vice versa."

I frowned in distaste. "Is something like that normal?"

"It's incredibly *ab*normal," Rune responded. "And markedly dangerous, to be honest — and that's just performing the rite. He could have died."

"I suppose you're wondering why anyone would do something like that," Endow chimed in.

"Actually, I'm not," I countered. "He did it for reasons already discussed: he wanted power. Oddly enough, Rune and I actually had a discussion recently about power and what people would do to obtain it, and the *sivrrut* of an Incarnate has to be the Holy Grail of power."

"That's actually not a bad analogy," Rune noted. "Anyway, in Static's case, even though the amulet gave him access to Gamma's power, he was worried that if he angered Mommy, she could punish him by taking his favorite new toy."

"And the rite was supposed to eliminate that threat," I concluded.

"The problem, however, is that humans aren't built to house those kinds of forces," Endow stated. "Static was no exception."

"It started eating him alive," I concluded. "That's why he looked the way he did, with the cadaverous face and skeletal body. The *sivrrut* in the amulet was devouring him."

"Yes," Endow agreed with a nod. "The way he presented himself when you first met the killer and when you fought him was his actual appearance. The semblance we typically saw was manufactured."

"Again, shouldn't you guys have noticed that?" I asked.

"Remember that glow he always had around him?" Rune chimed in. "Everyone always thought it was just an attribute of his power — and it may have started out that way — but it was really used to mask his appearance."

"So he fooled you," I stated in simple terms, reflecting on the fact that the secondary glow I'd once seen on Static had obviously emanated from his amulet.

"Hey, it wasn't like he just slapped on a handlebar mustache and started speaking with a fake French accent," Rune protested. "He put an enormous amount of power and effort into maintaining his façade, and — as you noted earlier — he had an actual Incarnate helping him. That alone made it a hard hill to climb in terms of seeing through the ruse."

"If we could get back on point?" Endow interjected. "We were discussing how Static bound himself to the amulet that Gamma had given him."

"I'm guessing Gamma found out at some point and wasn't happy," I said. "After all, the whole point of sharing her power was so she wouldn't see him die."

"That's what Cerek conveyed to Reverb," Rune reported. "However, Gamma couldn't take it back. Her power was now inextricably linked to Static's life force. If she took it back, it would kill him."

"So she came up with another solution," I said in a matter-of-fact tone. "She decided to kill herself."

# INCARNATION

## Chapter 60

Surprisingly, my statement wasn't as shocking as one might have expected. Endow merely nodded, giving me an appraising glance.

"True," she acknowledged. "Gamma did kill herself, but how did you know that?"

"Cerek told me," I answered. "It was in his clues."

"You know," Rune said, "you're getting an awful lot of information from two rinky-dink clues."

I laughed. "Just shows you brought in the right man for the job after all. But I can elaborate if you like."

"We insist," Rune stated drolly.

"Well," I began, "Cerek gave me two words as clues: MOUSES and KLEOP. The former was somewhat the more familiar of the two, so I started researching it first."

"And what did you find out?" Endow asked, plainly curious.

"The most salient point was that 'mouses' actually is acceptable as a plural of 'mouse,'" I replied.

"Excellent, detective," Rune chimed in. "You've cracked the case."

I ignored his jibe. "More obscure, however, is the fact that the same spelling in Greek is pronounced 'Moy-sis,'" I explained, enunciating the word for my audience. "It's a variation of 'Moses' — assuming you've heard that name before."

"We're familiar with the story," Endow assured me. "Please go on."

"Once I found that out," I continued, "I thought I had the answer. See, Moses means 'drawn from the water,' and we just happen to have an Incarnate whose attributes seemingly center on water."

"You thought Mariner was your guy," Rune surmised.

"Yeah," I acknowledged, "but I didn't point the finger right away because — even though I felt I was right — there was still a *chance* that I was wrong. Turns out I was, so I guess I owe him an apology."

Rune pooh-poohed my concerns. "You never actually accused him of anything, so no harm, no foul."

I wasn't sure I actually agreed with him, but continued with my narrative.

"The other clue, 'KLEOP,' initially threw me for a loop," I admitted. "However, sticking with the Grecian theme that began with the first clue, I found out that the name 'Cleopatra' begins with the letter $K$ in Greek."

Endow frowned in thought for a moment. "So you think that when Cerek wrote 'KLEOP,' he was intending to write 'Cleopatra'?"

I nodded. "Yes."

She looked at Rune, who shrugged, saying, "As you can tell from my responses to Jim's story about the clues, I've got no info on this subject. That's one of the few areas in which Cerek didn't share anything with Reverb."

"But there's still the question of why Cerek gave Greek renderings of the names," Endow noted. "And why didn't he finish spelling out Cleopatra?"

"I think I know the answer to that," I said. "But first, I'm going to go out on a limb here and say that Cerek was Greek."

"I believe that's right," Rune confirmed.

"Well, in my opinion, I think he panicked," I offered. "I couldn't reach him with my telepathy, but I could pick up on his emotional vibes when he was leaving the clues, and he was just a bundle of raw nerves. His anxiety level was in the stratosphere. As a result, I think he inadvertently reverted to Greek spellings of the clues he wanted to leave. As to why he didn't finish spelling Cleopatra, the short answer is that he probably ran out of time."

Rune gave me an inquisitive look. "What do you mean?"

"On those first two occasions when I saw Cerek, there was always this weird rumbling sound all around us. It wasn't until that second visit that I figured out what it was: snoring."

"Snoring?" Rune echoed in surprise.

"Yeah," I confirmed with a nod. "When I first figured it out, I assumed that it was Cerek — that he was projecting his astral form while asleep and the accompanying sound was some kind of side-effect. But when I ruminated on it, I recalled the snoring being interrupted that second time, as if the sleeper were coming awake. That's what seemed to make him panic. But if he were the sleeper, I couldn't figure out why coming awake would cause him dread."

"I suppose you discovered the answer?" Endow queried.

"I did," I answered, "but not until later, and it ties back into the clues."

"In what way?" asked Rune.

"In the story," I replied, "Moses is raised in the house of Pharaoh — the enemy who wanted him dead. That's what Cerek was telling me when he gave me the first clue. It had nothing to do with water; it was indicating that he was with the enemy. Or rather, the killer, Static.

Basically, he could only safely project his astral form — sneak out, so to speak — when Static was asleep. It was Static's snoring that I was hearing, and that's why Cerek panicked and took off without finishing the second clue. He needed to get back before Static woke up."

There was silence for a moment as the two Incarnates appeared to chew on my explanation.

"I don't know," Rune droned. "It sounds good, but it's a lot to base on two random clues."

"But they *weren't* random clues," I insisted. "When Cerek showed up that second time, I actually blurted out a couple of queries. Specifically, I asked him where he was, and I asked what happened to Gamma. The clues he gave were actually answers to my questions. With the hint about Moses, he told me his location: he was with the killer, as evidenced by the fact that he and Reverb came out of Static's amulet when I was fighting him."

"And with the Cleopatra clue, he was telling you what happened to Gamma," Endow remarked.

"Exactly," I intoned. "If there's one thing that everybody knows about Cleopatra, it's that she committed suicide. Somewhat less well known is the fact that, at one point, she made her son co-ruler of Egypt."

"She shared her power," Endow concluded. "So with that clue, Cerek told you everything you needed to know about what happened to Gamma."

"Almost," I countered. "I still don't know exactly how she died."

"Yes, you do," Rune countered. "We all do. We saw it when we confronted Static." He reached out and picked up the crystal relic from the table. "*This* is how she did it."

I glanced at the crystal that Static had used to create doubles of Rune, Endow, and Mariner, reflecting on what had happened then.

"So, you're saying she created a double of herself," I hypothesized, "and then had it take her life?"

"I'm not just saying it," Rune announced. "That's what happened — at least according to the information we got from Ursula and Reverb."

*Who, in turn, got it from Static and Cerek*, I thought. It ultimately meant that the info provided amounted to a lot of hearsay, but that didn't make it wrong. Moreover, I really didn't question the fact that Gamma took her own life; it was just the manner in which it happened.

"That said," Rune continued, "Reverb and Ursula got a lot of insight from their sources as to what led up to it."

"Basically," Endow added, "Gamma was both livid and frightened when she found out about the rite Static had performed. But, as you already know, she couldn't take her *sivrrut* back without killing him."

"Which was ironic because leaving him with her power was actually destroying him," I noted. "So she decided to kill herself, as I deduced before. Once she was dead, her power would dissipate — including what was in the relic Static had bonded with — and he'd go back to being a normal person. There might be some embarrassment over what had happened, but Gamma wouldn't be around to deal with it, and her son would survive."

"Close, but no cigar," Rune intoned. "In truth, Gamma actually thought that, given time, she could convince Static to reverse the rite, as it was the only way she thought he could survive. But later she found out that

Static had his own plans for survival, and they were a bit more radical than anything she ever would have contemplated."

"Basically, he planned to commit a murder here in Permovren," Endow said. "He would leave enough clues to implicate an Incarnate in the crime, and then wait for the one item to be brought here that could punish an Incarnate for such a crime."

"The Kroten Yoso Va," I guessed.

"Yes," Endow confirmed with a nod. "Static wanted to use it to siphon power from other Incarnates, which he could then use to cure himself, as well as wield as his own."

"But why go through all that instead of just reversing the rite?" I asked. "Seems like the end result and getting the Kroten Yoso Va are the same."

"Except the power from the Kroten Yoso Va would be much greater and wouldn't devour him," Endow stated. "Plus, if he successfully reversed the rite, Gamma was sure to take the amulet — and her power — back for good. He couldn't risk that."

"And on her part, Gamma saw death as a way to resolve a lot of problems," Rune noted. "First and foremost, her son would live; that's what was most important to her. In addition, he wouldn't be a murderer. And lastly, no one would die because of the things she'd done."

"So what went wrong?" I asked.

Rune sighed. "Everything."

I gave him a confused look. "You'll have to be more specific."

"Using the crystal, Gamma creates the double of herself and orders it to attack," he said. "All goes according to plan up until the point when she's about to die."

"Hold on," I said. "I recall when you guys reverse engineered her death, she didn't just go gently into that good night. She was fighting back."

"There's something about conflict that spurs the double to fight even more vigorously — energizes them," Endow remarked. "Something we learned firsthand. In Gamma's case, she wanted the fight to end quickly, so she fought back to a certain extent."

"And as I was saying," Rune chimed in, "it's at the point where she's about to die that she realizes something's wrong: her power's not dissipating — neither the portion that still resides with her nor the *sivrrut* in Static's relic."

I looked at him in surprise. "But that's what you told me happens when an Incarnate dies. Their power disappears."

"But it didn't," Rune stated. "Instead, all of Gamma's remaining power seemed to consolidate in Static's amulet. That's why she was shouting 'No' when we reverse engineered things."

"She was also shouting for Cerek," I noted, and then my eyes widened as realization hit. "Wait — he was with her. He was there when she died."

"That's right," Rune agreed. "And with the last of her power, she hid him in Static's relic."

"Which is why none of us were able to locate him," Endow said. "The *sivrrut* in the amulet obscured his presence."

"I'm thinking that was probably the point," I offered. "My guess is that he knew everything about the power-sharing arrangement between Gamma and Static.

Gamma probably realized that if she was gone and Static still had her power, Cerek was as good as dead."

"That's pretty much on the nose," Rune acknowledged.

"Actually, it's not completely clear that he would have killed Cerek," Endow confided. "He's had several *laamuffals* over the years find out his secret, and he usually just wiped their minds and sent them back."

"So they found out that the emperor had no clothes on," Rune mused. "That certainly explains why his turnover rate for *laamuffals* was so high."

"And he also had his mother looking over his shoulder back then," I noted. "Killing *laamuffals* probably would have cost him his one ally. And that brings to mind another question: does anyone know what happened to Gamma's body?"

"Yeah," Rune said. "It seems her double wasn't just supposed to kill Gamma, but totally expunge her — erase all trace of her."

"Apparently she didn't want her body to be found," Endow expounded, "since that might give some indication of what had happened."

I simply nodded in understanding at this, as it showed notable foresight on Gamma's part. Case in point: upon finding out why I was here, one of the first things I'd done was ask about Gamma's body.

"Anyway," Rune continued, "getting back to the subject of Gamma's power going to the relic, that was both a blessing and a curse for Static."

"How so?" I asked.

"It was a blessing in that he then had all her power," Endow explained. "Or as much of it as he could get in Permovren. It was a curse because now it was devouring him even faster."

"That being the case, he stepped up his timetable," Rune said.

I raised an eyebrow. "What timetable?"

"Murder," Endow said flatly.

"And this is what allowed him to do it," Rune announced, holding up the green crystal. "It permitted him to make doubles of Reverb and Pinion."

"Which, in the latter's case, killed him," Endow declared.

"I didn't think you guys could be killed by anything besides another Incarnate," I remarked. "That being the case, I have to ask: how many of those things" — I nodded toward the crystal — "do you folks have lying around?"

"Technically, the doubles it creates *are* Incarnates," Endow clarified, "so your supposition is right."

"As to how many of these there are," Rune added, "I'm hoping there's just the one. To be honest, I've never seen anything quite like this."

He stared at the crystal as he spoke, obviously intrigued.

"So where did it come from?" I inquired.

"According to Cerek, Gamma created it," Rune said. "From all indications, it was infused with her power, and that's actually what fueled this thing. In fact, her *sivrrut* is the only thing that can activate it. When she died, her power was supposed to disappear, thereby making this crystal inert."

"Only her power didn't disappear," Endow interjected. "And as a result, this stayed active and fully functional."

"And under the control of Static," I surmised, "who had her power and could therefore control it."

"Next thing you know, he's using it to kill Incarnates," Rune said, "in hopes that it would force me to bring forth the Kroten Yoso Va."

"Well, he didn't actually *kill* Reverb," I corrected. "And on that topic, how did Reverb actually survive?"

"As you can guess, Static made a double of him," Rune explained. "Initially he fought back, but that only seemed to strengthen his look-alike. Moreover, Reverb realized that the stronger he made his attacks, the more likely he was to kill someone innocent — even after he transported to the field outside the castle."

"And rather than kill someone, he just shut down," I guessed. "Stopped fighting back."

"Yes," Endow said. "And you can tell from his appearance that he suffered for it."

I nodded, shuddering internally at the thought of Reverb's limbless torso. "Will he be all right?"

"Believe it or not, he'll be fine," Rune assured me. "Although his effigy crumbled, Cerek somehow smuggled Reverb into the relic with him. He was near death, but Cerek used the *sivrrut* housed there to keep him alive."

"And it was during that time," I said, "while he was in the amulet with Cerek, that Reverb got a good chunk of the story."

"Correct," Rune confirmed.

"Any particular reason he never tried to let you guys know he wasn't dead?" I asked.

"He didn't even have the power to keep himself alive," Rune countered. "He had nothing to spare for reaching us."

I gave him a skeptical look. "So how's he alive now?"

"Shortly after you and Static disappeared, our doubles vanished," Endow explained. "We know now that occurred when you defeated Static, but immediately afterward we were able to get to Reverb and sustain him."

"He's strong enough now that he's taken over the healing process himself," Rune commented. "He's even regrown his limbs. Needless to say, his *laamuffal* Konstantin is overjoyed that he's still alive."

I nodded as Rune's statement brought to mind another thought. "That reminds me — what happened to Pinion's *laamuffal*?"

"He shut down after Pinion died," Endow informed me. "Apparently Pinion's *sivrrut* was the life force that animated him."

"And Cerek?" I asked. "How's he?"

Rune and Endow both went silent, which was an answer in and of itself.

"He didn't make it," Endow finally muttered solemnly. "That blow from Static killed him — probably intentionally." She looked frustrated for a moment and then added, "He should have just come to us."

I gave her a sympathetic look. "Like I said earlier, he was still trying to protect Gamma's son. Regardless, what would you guys have done if you'd found out about Static?"

"Probably attempt to strip him of Gamma's power," Rune admitted.

"And perhaps kill him in the process," I added. "Maybe that's why Cerek didn't come to any of you even after Reverb was attacked. If you ended up killing Static, it would have meant that Gamma died for nothing, which was probably the worst thing Cerek could have imagined."

There was silence for a moment as the two Incarnates seem to let my words sink in.

"Anyway, I think all of us pretty much know the rest of the story," Rune said. "Static comes after Jim in our suite, Jim outs him in front of us, and ultimately Jim takes him down *mano a mano*."

"Sounds simple when you put it like that," I observed. "It was a little more touch-and-go at the time. For instance, I wasn't sure Endow would back my play when I said I switched the evidence."

Endow smiled. "Neither did I, but I thought you deserved a chance. How'd you know Static was lying?"

"His emotions," I replied. "He was practically on the verge of panic. I can't read the rest of you, but it just struck me that a near-omnipotent being doesn't have much to panic about. In addition, it all seemed centered on my response — what I was going to say when he kept goading me to confess."

"For a moment there, I thought you were actually going to break down and admit it," Rune shared.

"Oddly enough, so did I," I admitted. "It was like there was a tiny voice in my head saying over and over that I should confess."

Unexpectedly, Endow and Rune exchanged another knowing glance.

"What?" I asked. "What are you two not saying?"

Rune cleared his throat before speaking. "Ahem. It's possible — likely, in fact — that when Static and you had your *tete-a-tete* in your brain, he planted that little compulsion to confess. Basically, if you had confessed, no one would have ever thought to question his analysis of the cog, which he never actually did."

I looked at him in bewilderment. "But if he wanted me to confess to something I didn't do, why send Ursula to kill me?"

"I should probably clarify," uttered Rune. "A compulsion along the lines we're talking about could actually have been used to make you do anything. In this instance, Static just attempted to utilize it to get a convenient confession. In truth, he could have originally intended to use it at some other time, for some other reason, but changed his mind."

"As for him trying to kill you," Endow chimed in, "that was really to make Rune bring out the Kroten Yoso Va."

"He knew that I'd brought you here and felt responsible for you," Rune admitted. "If you died, he thought the guilt would break down my resolve."

"Geez," I droned. "He really wanted that thing badly, didn't he?"

"Oh, yes," Endow concurred with a nod. "According to Ursula, it's why he started coming to the Cosmos Corridor regularly."

"Huh?" I muttered, baffled.

"Static had started entering the Cosmos Corridor more often lately," she explained. "He never stated what he wanted, but now we know: he was looking for some indication of where the Kroten Yoso Va was."

I dwelt on that for a moment. It would certainly explain why he was present the last time I went there (although I hadn't really given much thought to what he was doing when I showed up). If I hadn't been so focused on my own agenda, maybe I would have been more curious about what he was up to, although it probably didn't matter at this point.

"Getting back to him trying to kill me, did he just not consider that Ursula might fail?" I asked. "He just assumed she'd put me six feet under?'

"Actually, he just thought that she'd be able to catch you with your guard down," Endow responded. "Not to mention that he had a back-up plan."

I frowned. "What kind of back-up plan?"

Rune glared at Endow for a moment, then said, "You remember how the killer typically didn't leave any evidence at his crime scenes? Well—"

"Are you kidding me?!" I interjected as the truth became clear. "He was going to blast our suite to rubble? When were you planning to tell me — after I sat down on a stick of dynamite?"

"First of all, there wasn't any dynamite," Rune began. "And second, I found and disarmed the object he was planning to use, so you were never really in danger of getting blown up. So the only chance of something happening to you was if you got sloppy or distracted and let Ursula knife you."

"Speaking of whom," Endow muttered before I could respond.

At that moment, the door to the room opened and Ursula stepped in.

"Why didn't anybody tell me my boyfriend had dropped by?" she asked of no one in particular while giving me a wink.

# INCARNATION

## Chapter 61

"What are you doing up?" Endow admonished, coming to her feet, as did Rune and I. "You should be resting."

"I'm fine," Ursula insisted. "Static just messed around in my head, and that's a bit of a mess anyway."

Everyone snickered at that, at which point Ursula turned to me.

"You, sir, are a terrible first date," she declared. "Your response to my actions were over the top. A little knife in the heart never hurt anybody."

I chuckled heartily, saying, "I admit it's possible I overreacted."

"Well, lucky for you I like you," she droned, "so you'll get a second bite at the apple. Plus, it's slim pickings around here."

"Okay, that's enough out of you," Endow stated, marching over to Ursula and taking her by the elbow. "Come on, let's get you back into bed."

"Wait," she uttered, spinning toward me. "You'll come see me before you go?"

"Oh, uh, of course," I muttered. Her question had taken me a little by surprise, but with everything resolved, I supposed I would be leaving soon.

"I wouldn't take off without saying good-bye to you and Endow," I added.

"Who said anything about Endow?" Ursula demanded saucily. "You're aiming too high. Rune's not going to let you within a mile of this one." As she finished speaking, she hooked a thumb toward Endow.

She then gave me a playful wink as Endow said, "Okay, now I *know* you need some rest..."

She continued talking as she guided Ursula from the room, but I couldn't hear any more of what was said.

As Rune and I sat back down, I pulled the badge — which I happened to be wearing — from under my shirt and up over my head. (Oddly enough, after my battle with Static, I discovered that the chain had repaired itself.)

"I suppose you'll be wanting this back," I said, holding it out to him.

"The badge?" he asked.

"The Kroten Yoso Va," I corrected. He didn't move to take it, so I simply rested it on my thigh.

Rune merely stared at me for a moment. "When did you figure it out?"

"Right before Static tried to take it," I answered. "He mentioned something about the items he was taking from me being in good hands. It triggered some things in my memory that you had said — like how Ursula was in good hands with me. How you and the other Incarnates were in good hands with me. You seemed to be equating me with 'good hands.' And that's where you also said the Kroten Yoso Va was: in good hands."

"That's really impressive," he said solemnly.

"Well, you dropped enough hints. I just didn't catch on until Static was about to get it, and suddenly it all became clear."

"No, what's really impressive is that I wasn't trying to drop any hints, but you figured it out anyway."

I blinked in surprise. "So it was just sheer luck that I happened to realize what that badge really was?"

"Even if you hadn't realized what it was, I'm not sure that the outcome would have been different."

245

"Other than me goading Static into taking it," I said. "Once he did that, it stripped him of his powers. Or rather, stripped him of *Gamma's* power."

"And in a way that didn't kill him," Rune noted. "Regardless, after his powers were gone, the doubles he'd manufactured vanished, along with anything else he'd created — including the compulsion in your mind."

"That's nice to know," I blurted out in relief as a new question popped up in my brain. "Hmmm. Why do you think he never made a double of *me*?"

"Ursula might be able to confirm it with what she got from his brain," Rune began, "but I'm guessing Static was worried about overtaxing the crystal."

"What do you mean?"

"He'd already used it to make doubles of three Incarnates," Rune explained. "That was seemingly more than he'd ever done at one time."

"Yeah," I agreed with a nod. "Before that, he was picking you guys off one at a time."

"Right," Rune conceded. "He only made three doubles out of desperation — at the point when he'd been unmasked as the killer. If he'd known the crystal could manage that earlier, there would probably be more of us dead. That said, I think he was still concerned about overworking it — not to mention the fact that, on the surface, you shouldn't have presented much of a challenge."

"In other words, he thought he could handle me without using up a bunch of *sivrrut*."

"You said it yourself earlier," Rune stated with a laugh. "Our arrogance would be our undoing. Guess you were right."

"Normally I'd be overjoyed about taking you pompous showboats down a notch," I deadpanned, causing Rune to chuckle. "At the moment, though, I'm trying to figure out if I'm angry with you or not."

His eyebrows went up in surprise. "About what?"

"About sticking me with the Kroten Yoso Va without telling me. About making me its Keeper without saying a word about it. In fact, you told me that you didn't even bring it here."

"Of course I brought it here!" he shot back. "Do I look stupid? We had an Incarnate killer on our hands. Why would I leave behind the one thing that could definitely stop him?"

"So all that talk about not wanting to use it on your friends was just that — talk?"

"No, all that was true. The only area where I fibbed a little was in saying that I hadn't brought it to Permovren."

"Well, it would have been nice if you had told me the truth. Letting me walk around with it was like putting a target on my back."

"It only made you a target if people knew you had it, and no one did," Rune stated. "Do you remember when you first encountered the Kroten Yoso Va and touched it?"

"How could I forget? It barbecued my hands – punishment for grabbing it."

Rune shook his head. "It wasn't punishing you. It was *forging* you."

I looked at him in confusion. "Forging me into what?"

"Keeper, of course," Rune said matter-of-factly.

"Wait a minute," I muttered, frowning. "Are you saying you selected me as Keeper back when I first touched the Kroten Yoso Va?"

Rune stared at me for a moment, then sighed. "I really haven't done a great job of explaining this to you."

"To be honest," I countered, "you haven't done *any* kind of job of explaining *anything*. In fact, if this were an actual job, you would have bombed the interview."

"Well, let me provide some clarity," he offered. "Ninety-nine times out of a hundred, Incarnates select the person to be Keeper – usually an individual with an advanced degree of mystical or magical knowledge."

"And that hundredth time?" I asked.

"On that occasion, the Kroten Yoso Va makes the selection."

"Hold on," I said, blinking in bewilderment. "Are you trying to say that artifact somehow picked me to be Keeper?"

"I think it did more than that," Rune stated.

"Like what?"

Rune appeared to reflect for a few seconds, then said, "As you can imagine, there are times when the Kroten Yoso Va is without a Keeper. For instance, if the Keeper dies and no successor is found. There are also occasions when it's simply been lost or misplaced. During those times, when it's essentially homeless, the artifact can often be used by anyone who is well-versed in the mystic arts. But when you first came across it, the Kroten Yoso Va was in the hands of Diabolist Mage, who was – at best – a second-rate magician."

"Yeah, but the Kroten Yoso Va helped him elevate his game," I added, recalling how the artifact had allowed the Diabolist to cause destruction on an epic scale.

"That's my point," Rune stated. "The Diabolist wasn't enough of an adept to be able to use the Kroten Yoso Va. It never should have worked for him."

# INCARNATION

"So why did it?"

"Honestly, I think it was to get to you."

My eyes bulged in surprise. "What?"

"Think about it. You came across the Kroten Yoso Va because you were trying to find out who was behind all of the wanton destruction taking place. If it hadn't worked for the Diabolist, you wouldn't even know it existed."

"So it manipulated people and events in order to get what it wanted – a new Keeper."

I felt myself growing angry. This was very similar to an experience I'd had with the other Triumvirate Relic I'd encountered – the Beobona – which had also seemingly influenced events in order to obtain a desired outcome. Needless to say, I didn't like being maneuvered like a piece on a chessboard, feeling like my life wasn't my own.

"You say 'Keeper' like it's a bad word," Rune noted, interrupting my thoughts. "Don't you realize this is a rare and exceptional honor?"

"Ha!" I snorted derisively. "You'd feel differently if it was your life getting controlled, and your hands getting burned off."

"I can assure you that your life is still your own," Rune declared. "The Kroten Yoso Va won't keep you from drinking and driving, picking up hitchhikers, or making a host of other poor decisions. In short, your life is still yours, and – just like everybody else – you still have the ability to screw it up in a million different ways."

Not sure what to say, I merely grunted response.

"As to your hands getting burned," he continued, "do you remember how they were restored to their normal condition?"

I frowned for a moment, then said flatly, "The Kroten Yoso Va."

"Correct," he said with a nod. "It healed you. In fact, if you'd held on when you first touched it, your hands would have been whole when the artifact was done. Truth be told, you actually shouldn't have been able to let go until it had finished."

"Really?" I droned, sarcastically. "Well, now I feel bad for not holding on and letting it scorch my hands to the bone."

"As I said before, that wasn't to punish you."

"Yes, I know," I shot back. "It was to bestow some great and wonderful privilege on me, with the mild drawback of making me the target of a killer."

"Again, no one knew you had it. Because you had touched the Kroten Yoso Va and been selected as Keeper, it could be harmonized, so to speak, with your life force. Basically, it could be hidden on your person without anyone — even an Incarnate — realizing exactly what it was. They might detect something mystical about you, but they wouldn't be able to specifically identify it. And around here, the mystical is common."

"This is making more sense now," I said. "I'm starting to understand why you picked me to run point on this Gamma situation, and it's got nothing to do with my detective skills or you not being able to protect a normal person. It's because you could use me to hide the Kroten Yoso Va."

"In truth, that's only part of the reason," he admitted. "I honestly did have faith in your sleuthing ability."

"Let's say that's true," I said. "I'm still not hearing anything to justify not telling me about it."

"All right, there is something else," Rune admitted. "If you knew the truth, I was a little afraid of someone being able to get into your head and root it out, although that was unlikely."

"And why's that?"

"Because the Kroten Yoso Va bestows certain protections on its Keeper."

"Such as making it impossible for an Incarnate to take it by force."

"Exactly, but the protections go further than that. For instance, having it on you is one reason why Static's compulsion probably failed."

"Understood, but the killer didn't necessarily have to take it from me. He could have just murdered me to keep the Kroten Yoso Va from being used on him. Or, setting all that aside, he could have just lashed out at me if he thought I was getting too close to figuring things out."

"Well, let me put your mind at ease," Rune said. "You'll be happy to know that Endow and I placed additional protections around you in addition to the Kroten Yoso Va, so the killer couldn't just strike you down with a lightning bolt, open a crevasse under your feet, or anything like that. Satisfied?"

I was about to make a smart-aleck response when the door opened and Endow came back in. She quickly rejoined us and took her seat as before.

"So, what are we talking about?" she asked.

I simply stayed quiet, looking at Rune.

"It's okay," Rune finally said. "You can speak freely in front of her."

"Great," I said a little flippantly. "Your boyfriend was just explaining why he let me walk around with a giant bull's-eye on my back in the form of the Kroten Yoso Va."

"Wait," Endow muttered with a frown. "Boyfriend?"

She gave Rune a look that was equal parts hilarity and befuddlement.

"Yeah," I said. "The way you two are always hanging out, chatting together, and so on. It's pretty obvious how you feel about each other."

Endow put a hand up to her mouth, trying to suppress a fit of giggling. Rune, on the other hand, suddenly had a stern look on his face.

"Okay," he grumbled, leaning forward. "I'm going to advise you to stop before you embarrass yourself, junior. You don't know what you're talking about."

I raised an eyebrow. "You're saying I'm wrong?"

"I'm saying you've impressed us with your detective skills. Don't make us go back and reevaluate."

"Fine," I stated. "I know how to settle this."

I turned to Endow, who had just regained her composure. Smiling, she suddenly sat up straight as she realized I was about to address her.

"Endow," I began, "tell the truth with no equivocating or dancing around the question: how do you feel about Rune?"

Endow seemed on the verge of having another fit of giggling, but then she got herself under control and cleared her throat. "Ahem. I think that Rune is weird and eccentric, often outlandish, occasionally freaky, and always inscrutable. But I love him deeply and would do anything for him, just as I know he loves and would do anything for me."

I gave Rune a smug look. "So, I'm wrong, huh?"

Ignoring me, Rune simply looked at Endow and said, "Really? That's how you're going to leave it?"

She simply gave him a big grin and shrugged.

# INCARNATION

"Unbelievable," Rune muttered, shaking his head in exasperation. Turning to me, he said, "Okay, I'm going to fix this with three simple words, and when I'm done, we're not going to talk about this anymore."

"Sure thing," I agreed. "So what are the three words? That you love her?"

Rune gave me a steely look and declared, "She's my sister."

# INCARNATION

## Chapter 62

It seemed as though Endow was never going to stop laughing after Rune's comment. I simply sat there, cheeks turning red, as a lot of things suddenly became clear. Whenever he had made comments about staying away from Endow, it wasn't in the vein of a jealous paramour; it was in the context of a protective older brother. (Or perhaps younger brother. Regardless, after my faux pas in regard to their relationship, I didn't care to delve any more into the subject.)

"Well, Sherlock," Rune said after a minute or two, "any more keen and brilliant observations you want to make?"

"Just that you guys really need to get that nepotism policy in place," I noted.

"We'll take it under advisement," Rune stated without much enthusiasm. "Now that the sidebar conversations are out of the way, we need to ask you something."

"Sure," I said, happy to move on to another subject.

"Do you recall when you went exploring and I couldn't find you?" asked Rune.

I nodded, saying, "Yeah."

"Where exactly were you then?" he inquired.

I shrugged. "Some room — pitch black on the inside. I couldn't see anything, even when I cycled my vision through the spectrum."

"What happened while you were in there?" Endow chimed in.

"What happened?" I echoed. "Nothing. I couldn't see anything, didn't know where I was, so I left —

although, to be honest, it was more like the room shoved me through the exit."

Rune frowned. "About how long do you think you were in that room?"

I shrugged. "A couple of minutes, maybe. Like I said, I couldn't see anything, so there was nothing to hang around for."

Rune and Endow looked at each other for a moment, then the former said, "Relatively speaking, there were at least a couple of hours when I couldn't find you. We think you were in that room during that time."

I looked at them in confusion. "A couple of hours? No, that's not possible."

"We think you were in the Room of Ebon Enlightenment," Endow remarked.

"I recall Ursula mentioning something about it," I stated. "But she didn't have a lot of details, just something about it answering questions you don't know you have."

"Like maybe figuring out that you're carrying something that you didn't know was on your person?" Rune suggested.

I didn't say anything, choosing instead to reflect for a moment on what he was suggesting — that a purported visit to the Room of Ebon Enlightenment had resulted in me learning about my badge being the Kroten Yoso Va. It was possible, I suppose...

"Anyway," Rune continued, "now that the major crisis is over, we need to address some things that happened while you've been here."

"Such as?" I queried.

"You've bestowed gifts in the Cosmos Corridor," Endow noted. "You've infiltrated one of the Four Frescos.

255

You've also entered the Room of Ebon Enlightenment. These are all privileges granted solely to Incarnates."

"I'm sorry," I said sincerely. "I honestly didn't know I was breaking any rules. Well, maybe with the gifts in the Cosmos Corridor I *suspected* that—"

"Jim, you're misunderstanding," Rune stated, cutting me off. "It's not that Incarnates are the only ones *permitted* to do those things; it's that Incarnates are the only ones who *can* do those things."

"In other words," Endow clarified, "it's impossible for anyone else to do them."

"I don't understand," I muttered, shaking my head in confusion, as if clearing out cobwebs. "What are you trying to say?"

"Isn't it obvious, Jim?" asked Rune. "*You* are an Incarnate!"

THE END

# INCARNATION

Thank you for purchasing this book! If you enjoyed it, please feel free to leave a review on the site from which it was purchased.

Also, if you would like to be notified when I release new books, please subscribe to my mailing list via the following link:   http://eepurl.com/C5a45

Finally, for those who may be interested in following me, I have included my website and social media account info:

Website: http://www.kevinhardmanauthor.com/

BookBub:    https://www.bookbub.com/authors/kevin-hardman

Amazon: https://amazon.com/author/kevinhardman

Facebook: www.facebook.com/kevin.hardman.967

Twitter: @kevindhardman